THE WEAKER SEX

Slowly, she moved her hands up from her thighs to her throat. Without shifting them away from the frothy fabric of what she wore—her actions un-subtly erotic as her pale fingers trailed up and over her body, she located the tie fastening at the neck-line of the garment. She suddenly unfastened it, then shrugged her shoulders and spread wide her arms. And the nightgown was seen to be more like a coat then a dress, so that the woman was at once naked at the front from her throat to where her knees were on the ground. Her slender body as pale as her face.

"I think you understand this, Edge?" she said breathlessly. "You know what is required of you. As a hired man, hired by *me*, you have to do as I tell you, and I am telling you to . . ."

The plan was well underway.

THE EDGE SERIES:

Best-Selling Series!

#44 The Most Violent Westerns in Print

EDGE

THE BLIND SIDE

BY

George G. Gilman

PINNACLE BOOKS NEW YORK

EDGE #44: THE BLIND SIDE

Copyright©1984 by George G. Gilman

All rights reserved, including the right to reproduce this book or portions thereof in any form.

Pinnacle Books edition, published for the first time in the U.S.A.

First printing, February 1984

ISBN: 0-523-42042-0

Can. ISBN: 0-523-43112-0

Cover illustration by Bruce Minney

Printed in the United States of America

PINNACLE BOOKS, INC.
1430 Broadway
New York, New York 10018

9   8   7   6   5   4   3   2   1

For F.H.
another lady who
provides the proof.

THE BLIND SIDE

Chapter One

Edge rasped an inarticulate sound and reined to a halt the pair of mules and the buckboard, wound the reins around the brake lever and dug the makings from a pocket of his shirt. Then, while he rolled, lit and took a first drag against the cigarette, he watched the activity at the side of the much larger rig that was stalled on the trail about a half mile ahead.

It was a covered wagon that needed at least two animals in the traces, but this morning just one of the horses which had hauled the rig out to this point on the Calendar-to-Tuscon trail was ready and willing to face up to another day's work in the heat and glare of the south-western sun—the obedient chestnut standing patiently beside the wagon while a man and a woman attempted vainly to stir the gray, sprawled on its side, into at least rising to his feet.

The couple had made night camp where the trail started to rise up off a broad area of scrub desert and twist through the Gila Mountains—had left the wagon parked on the trail and built

their fire, hobbled the horses and bedded down
on a lushly grassed patch of ground between it
and a partially tree-fringed waterhole.

Now, in his efforts to coax the obstinate gray
into rising, the man carried a skillet to the hole,
filled it with water and brought it back to offer
to the animal. And, while he was gone the few
yards—his back to the scene—the woman
directed a vicious kick at the belly of the horse.
The mistreatment resulted in a frail motion of
the tail, and the setting down of the skillet of
water caused the gray to drag its head away.

Edge had momentarily scowled at the ill-
tempered action of the woman, but his features
were again in their usual impassive set when he
took up the reins, flicked them languidly over
the backs of the mules and vented another
grunt to start the team and buckboad moving.

The face of the man was of the kind that divided opinion between ugliness and handsome-
ness—those who considered him ruggedly attractive were unworried by a certain quality of
latent cruelty that could perhaps be seen in the
line of the thin lips and the icily cold light of the
eyes. The eyes were light blue and were always
narrowed to slits beneath their hooded lids.
Above and dropping sharply down to either
side of his wide mouth he affected just the
merest indication of a moustache. And these
two features—the blueness of the eyes and the
style of the moustache—provided the least
subtle clues to the mixture of blood in his veins
that made him a half-breed: he was in fact the

son of a Mexican father and a Swedish mother.

Born to them a little over forty years ago and showing it—and showing, too, that there had been few easy times during his life. This seen in the narrow-eyed, thin-lipped face that was long and lean and cloaked with skin darkened as much by exposure to the elements as by heritage; and networked with countless deep lines inscribed by the experiences of as well as the passing of the years. There was little of his brow to be seen because of the unruly, jet black hair that escaped from under his hat to fall across it. The cheekbones were prominent beneath the slits of his eyes and the sparsely fleshed, time-scarred skin was stretched taut down to his firm jawline. There was a hawkishness about the shape of his nose, and the nostrils were flared. He had the kind of beard that made it seem like he needed to shave thirty minutes after he already had. This morning, it was three hours since his sun-up shave and his lower face was already sprouting bristles—many gray ones among those of darker hue. There was much less sign of graying among the black hair that framed the stoic face, worn long enough for the ends to brush his shoulders at either side.

Shoulders that were broad, but by no means massively so—just as his chest did not bulge with muscle, nor his arms. And his waist was narrow, his belly flat. He perhaps looked long legged. But, on the whole, at six feet three inches tall and weighing about two hundred

pounds, he seemed to be leanly in proportion
and gave an impression of being quietly strong
without commanding any obvious brute
strength.

Another impression he gave on this sun-
bright, clear-skied and suddenly tension-
riddled morning was of being a down-at-heel
no-hoper. For his garb was a match for his apparently unshaven and uncertainly trail dusty
face—a black Stetson with a plain band, a gray
shirt, black denim pants, black riding boots
and a brown leather gunbelt with a Frontier
Colt in the holster that he did not have tied
down to his right thigh while he was riding a
rig rather than a horse. An upper portion of his
red longjohns was visible above the top button
of his open shirt, and around his unkerchiefed
neck there was a string of dull-coloured wooden
beads. Every item of his outfit was old and
worn, sweat stained and dirty with trail dust,
scuffed or scratched, torn and sometimes
mended, fitting well enough but completely
lacking in style.

Likewise the Western saddle, accoutrements
and Winchester rifle that comprised the only
freight on the rear of the buckboard. And the
elderly buckboard, too, which had bleached and
warped timbers, rusted ironwork and a badly
repaired off-side rear wheel.

Not so the mules, though. Which, to the nervous gazes of the man and the woman beside
the stalled covered wagon looked to be the only
possessions of the tall, lean, impassive

stranger on which he lavished any care. But they were in no position to see that the six-shooter in his holster and the repeater rifle in the boot of his saddle were perhaps old—but were not fogotten. And they could have no idea that from the rear of the string of beads around the stranger's neck there hung a sheath in which nestled a razor with a blade that was never allowed to become dulled.

"Morning to you, ma'am," Edge greeted in an even tone, raising a brown skinned hand to touch the broad, curved brim of his hat. "You plan to shoot me, feller?"

He had closed the distance from a half to a quarter mile when the woman spotted his approach and called the attention of the man to it —and the man lunged around the unwilling horse to reach the front of the wagon, snatched a rifle off the foot rest and whirled back into full view to aim it from the shoulder along the trail. Then remained rock steady in this attitude until Edge spoke and once more halted the mules and buckboard, the totally indifferent animals perhaps a hundred feet from the rear of the stalled wagon.

"If you intend harm to my wife and I, sir, I will not hesitate to put a bullet in your heart," the man answered, speaking English as only the most educated English spoke it in the half-breed's experience.

With the hand he had used to touch the brim of his Stetson, Edge took the cigarette from a corner of his mouth, got rid of its dead ash and angled it off his bottom lip again. Drew against it and expelled some smoke on a sigh before he replied: "I have to tell you—"

"Helen and I will always listen to rational argument, sir."

"I have to tell you," Edge went on as if there had been no interruption, "that if once you aim the rifle away from me don't point it towards me again. Unless you squeeze the trigger. For I sure as hell will do my best to kill you. One of the few things that rile me these days—having a gun aimed at me."

"Geoffrey?" The woman said, sounding as nervous as she looked—unable to tear her fixed gaze from the quietly spoken, disreputable-looking man on the buckboard. Her intonation added the query that asked her husband to do something, without offering any suggestions as to what this could be. She sounded as upper-crust English as the man.

"I sense, sir, that you have something else you wish to say to Helen and I?"

Edge shifted his cold eyed gaze from the man, to the woman who had backed off to stand alongside him and then at the gray gelding stretched out on the grass, neck and legs extended to their fullest extent, saliva trickling through his bared and gritted teeth and eye half hidden by the haw.

"The animal, sir?"

"You own him, feller?"

"Geoffrey and I are not horse thieves!"

"Did he have an open wound?" Edge looked

from the distressed animal to the man and
back again, ignoring the woman whose nervousness was giving way to displeasure.

"He became snagged on a cactus when we
were halted for tea last afternoon," the man
answered, his anxiety taking a different turn.

"Such a small cut on the leg of the animal
could not—" the woman started.

"Got infected through it," Edge cut in on the
woman. "Horse has all the signs of tetanus.
Which out here, a lot of miles from the closest
veterinarian, is sure to be fatal, feller. Since
he's your animal, you ought to end his misery."

"What?" the Englishman asked, and swallowed hard—glanced across the front of his
wife toward the doomed gelding but did not
allow the rifle to waver off target.

"Tetanus, feller. Maybe you people know it
as lockjaw, which is a very painful thing to—"

"I know what tetanus is, sir. But I've never
killed any—"

"So I have to figure you ain't going to blast a
bullet into me," Edge cut in as he wound the
reins around the brake lever, turned on the seat
and slid his Winchester out of the boot on the
saddle in the rear of the buckboard. Then, ap-
pearing to totally ignore the couple by the
stalled wagon, he swung down off the rig and
had the repeater angled across the front of his
body and pointed at the sky as he thumbed
back the hammer from a breech which already
contained a bullet.

"Geoffrey?" the woman said in the same

tone as before, or perhaps a little more stident-
ly, as she reached out a hand to grasp at the
forearm behind the hand that was cupped
under the rifle barrel.

"And you're Helen, ma'am," the half-breed
said, aware that he could have swung the
Winchester down and raked it to the aim while
the Englishman was momentarily off guard.
"For a lot of years now, I've been Edge. Figure
ain't any of us glad to know us yet. But then we
don't know us, do we?"

The English couple watched the half-breed
with a blend of horrified fascination mixed in
with perplexity as he closed with the pros-
trated gelding, altering the angle at which he
carried his rifle and gradually softening his
tone until he was almost whispering. Then he
came to an easy halt and was silent.

"Goeffrey?" Helen said shrilly.

"Shut your stupid mouth, Helen," her husband rasped, his tone harsher than that of
Edge but his voice no louder.

The gelding chomped and tried to swallow.
His ears pricked forward and he made a pitiful
attempt to rise, but it seemed as if every joint
in his body was locked solid. He whinnied.
Which was when the half-breed stepped across
his head, arced the rifle down so that the muzzle almost touched the animal's half-hidden
eyeball, and exploded a bullet into him.

"Geoffrey!" the woman shrieked, at her loud-
est yet in anger. "He shot our horse. He killed
Brutus!"

"Never give animals names, lady," Edge advised as he turned away from the gelding that was shuddering as the nervous system reacted to the death of the brain. "When they die, it doesn't come so hard."

He pumped the lever action of the Winchester to jack a fresh shell into the breech as the spent case was ejected. And then he eased the hammer gently forward as he canted the barrel to his shoulder, gripping the rifle around the frame in just one second. All this apparently done with a nonchalant indifference to his surroundings. But he had seen that the horse was certainly dead, the other half of the pair was not overly disturbed by the gunshot, the gunsmoke and the killing of one of its own kind, the woman was perhaps on the verge of hysterical anger and—most important of all—her husband had lowered his Winchester rifle from its aim at Edge.

"The poor, wretched creature," Helen wailed, having glanced at her husband's face and seen with the knowledge of experience she could expect no sympathy in a display of temper tantrum—so switching to a hastily summoned exhibition of grief on the brink of tears. "We might have been able to save him. I loved that horse, Geoffrey."

"Yeah, ma'am," the half-breed murmured as he dropped down on his haunches so that he could pick up the skillet with his free hand and raise it to his lips to drink of the warm but fresh water from the nearby hole. "And I saw from back there—" He gestured with the skillet along the trail in back of where the buckboard and mule stood. "—how the horse got a kick out of you."

Chapter Two

"You have eaten breakfast, sir?" the Englishman asked, after he glanced down at the rifle in
his hands, appeared to be embarrassed that he
was still holding it and then hurried to stow it
back under the seat of the covered wagon.

He was about the same age as Edge, an inch
or so shorter and weighed a good deal less. He
had a clean-shaven face with soft-looking skin
that was evenly shaded to a darker than natural color by the sun it was not usually exposed
to. He had reddish hair and clear green eyes, a
full-lipped mouth and very even teeth. Probably he had been classically handsome before
his nose suffered a break that had left it crooked as it healed. This blemish also added character to features which maybe before had lacked it. He wore good quality clothing—a Stetson, shirt, vest, pants and boots which were all
black—that was ideally suited to the kind of
rough country traveling in which he was en-
gaged, all of it purchased fairly recently so that
the newness was just beginning to be worked
out of the fabrics. His hands, and the arms

above bared by having the shirt sleeves rolled up, looked as soft and unused to the outdoor life as did the man's face.

"Best part of three hours ago, I figure," Edge replied to his question. "Looks like you people are headed in the same direction as I am."

"Coincidence can be as unkind as often as it can be kind," the woman put in acidly before her husband could respond.

She was a little younger than the men, no more than two or three years. Dressed in a country rather than a city style, but in an overly frilled white gown, smartly heeled blue shoes and paler blue hat with a too-broad brim which comprised the kind of store-bought outfit a farmer's wife or daughter might wear for a church social or Fourth of July picnic. And this woman, who was obviously not the wife of a farmer nor probably was the daughter of one, looked good in the clothes. For she had a brand of pale and delicate beauty of face and fragile slenderness of build that was perfectly complemented by the style and texture and colors of what she wore. She was no taller than five feet three inches and could not weigh much over a hundred pounds, the slightness of her build giving her a degree of womanly sexuality that few of her gender, with far more pronounced curves, could have matched. Likewise, the almost doll-like perfection of her oval shaped face with its blue eyes, snub nose, rosebud lips and milk white, flawless skin—in a frame of rich-growing, smoothly waved, honey-colored hair that swung to within a half inch of brushing her shoulders—had an undeniable sensuality that had to be lurking covertly just beneath the veneer of girlish innocence that was the first impression implied by her face.

Yes, Edge decided as he looked away from the sour-toned, scowling Helen after biting back on an intended response to her barbed comment: she was aging well, but what was on the inside of her carefully preserved shell was definitely suffering from the ravages of years that were totalling close to forty.

"Looking at the springs on the wagon, the rig is loaded heavy, feller?"

"A road agent, Geoffrey! Didn't I say when I first saw him coming toward us that I thought—"

"Ma'am?" Edge cut in, venting the single word as part of a sigh.

"Yes?"

"I don't like you."

"Well!" she stuttered as little more than a strangled gasp as she wrenched her shocked gaze from the impassive face of the half-breed to the startled and perhaps ready-to-be-afraid countenance of her husband. Then managed to squeal: "Geoffrey?"

Edge took another mouthful of water from the skillet, then spat it out like he was rinsing off a bad taste as he straightened up from the crouch beside the head of the dead horse. He canted the Winchester to his left shoulder, tip-

ped the water from the skillet to the ground
and extended the utensil toward the woman—
who moved even closer to her husband, and
clutched his upper arm this time, her pale and
slender hand formed into a claw.

"Guess you never will forget your name, will
you feller? Mine's Edge, or did I tell you that
once already?"

The Englishman nodded, his features set in a
grimace now. But he made no attempt to pull
free of the painful grip of his wife's talon-like
hand. "While you were trying to soothe the
horse, Mr. Edge. At least, I assume you were
talking merely for the sake of the animal you
were about to put down."

Edge nodded tersely. "That's right, feller.
And there ain't many occasions I talk just for
somebody to hear the sound of my voice. You
and your wife going to listen to what I have to
say now? Or will I just get back on the buckboard and leave the pair of you to kill your
other animal?"

"Did I not tell you earlier that Helen and I
will listen to good sense?" the Englishman
answered, his confidence rising as he realized
his feeling about the stranger had been correct
from the start. And, as if to emphasize that he
was now disassociating himself from those
opinions of his wife which he should never even
have considered in the first place, he gripped
her firmly around the waist to jerk her clawed
hand off his arm.

"Fine," the half-breed acknowledged after allowing the woman time to voice a complaint —but she remained in tight-lipped silence after her husband had directed a plea rather than a glower at her. "You have a rig that looks to be near overloaded. And just one animal to haul it through the hill country that's between here and wherever you're going. Now it so happens that I'm heading through the same hill country, feller. On a rig carrying just me and my gear, hauled by two healthy mules. So it seems horse sense to me that we should join forces?"

"Horse something!" the woman snapped.

"Helen!" her husband snapped, genuinely shocked by the implied crudity.

"No, ma'am," the half-breed countered evenly. "Horse sense it what it is, that it's to the benefit of your gelding. I'm like you, in one way. Much rather move on alone. But since I like most animals better than I like most people, I needed to speak on behalf of—"

"How much will you charge for the hire of your mules, Mr. Edge?" the Englishman interrupted.

"A ride aboard your wagon, feller."

There was a gleam of mistrust in the green eyes of the man for a moment. Then he took a forward step and thrust out his right hand as he said: "We have a bargain, sir. My wife and I are making for the town of Tucson. But if there is an opportunity for us to purchase a replace-

ment team animal before we get to our destination, I will so do and you may suit yourself
what you do then."

"Usually do," Edge replied as he shook the
recently roughened, patently strong hand of
the Englishman.

"You'll regret this, Geoffrey, I know you
will," the woman warned morosely.

"You have a given name, Mr. Edge? Please
call me Geoff. It's only Helen who insists upon
referring to me by the full—"

"Edge is the only one I have these days,
feller," the half-breed answered as he moved
away from the covered wagon. The Englishman was surprised by the move and had to
hurry to catch up.

"So, Edge it is then." Since the handshake to
seal the deal and his decision to trust the half
-breed, the man's mood had lightened to something akin to glee—like he welcomed the
stranger for the company he provided as much
as for the necessary help he was offering.

"You will continue to call me by your odd
pronunciation of *marm, Edge!*" the woman
called after the men as they moved from the
covered   wagon   toward   the   buckboard,
stressing the courtesy title and then his name
to make sure it did not sound like a diminutive.
"Or Mrs. Rochford, if you will!"

"Helen!" Geoffrey Rochford tossed back
over his shoulder, and he sounded like and wore
the expression of an indulgent and very patient
father mildly rebuking an intractable but much

adored offspring. Then he smiled wanly at the half-breed and lowered his voice to a whisper as he excused: "I'm sorry. At times, my wife can get the very devil in her."

Edge spat down at the trail as he halted at the side of the mules in the traces of the buckboard and then growled: "So maybe I'll call her Hel for short."

Chapter Three

Geoffrey and Helen Rochford lived in the county of Oxfordshire in England. And were taking what Rochford called a grand tour of the United States of America and her Territories. They were in coal mining, iron smelting and railroads—or rather, the man's family was in those businesses. Geoffrey Rochford was a self-confessed drone—which, the half-breed deduced for himself, was the English equivalent of a goldbrick.

"My family pay me handsomely to stay away from where they make their fortunes in the north of England, Edge. And I am only too happy to do so—provided the fortunes continue to be made so that they may afford still to pay me handsomely to stay away. If you get what I am getting at, sir?"

"No sweat, feller."

"Meaning what, Mr. Edge?" Helen Rochford asked, her sneering cynicism even more blatant when contrasted with her husband's jovial enthusiasm in denegrating himself.

The covered wagon was rolling through the

low-ridged Gila Mountains now, and perhaps thirty minutes had elapsed since they had left the campsite at the waterhole—where probably the coyotes and the buzzards were already preparing to feast on the carcass of the grey gelding. And would maybe later rest to digest the meal in the shade of the abandoned buckboard.

By adapting some of the harness from the buckboard, it had been a relatively simple and quick chore to attach the surviving horse at the front with the two mules at the back in the traces of the wagon. While this was being done, the woman climbed elegantly into the rear of the wagon, complaining about the increasing heat and glare from the sun and the nuisance of the flies which from time to time rose up from the gory eye wound of the horse to explore for pickings on the living animals and the exposed flesh of the humans. There in the shade and seeming coolness of the canvas stretched taut over the bows and tightly fastened at the rear behind her, Helen Rochford was silent.

"She generally takes a nap mid-morning and in the afternoon," was how her husband explained her withdrawal. He spoke this in a whisper and then, as he followed the halfbreed's instructions and helped with the harness adaptation and putting the animals in the traces, took pains to mute everything he did, steeling himself for a snarled rebuke each time he made a clumsy sound or one of the team broke the silence. This while Edge made no concessions toward allowing the woman a

period of undisturbed rest—but neither did he
purposely cause any unnecessary noise. For
quietly was how he did everything, unless the
situation called for a different approach.

When the wagon was ready to roll, Rochford
hurried to be first up on the seat—and peered
through the gap of the front opening to warn:
"We're leaving now, dear."

"I think it will be difficult for you to make
any more din while we are moving than you did
while we were still," she replied bitterly.

Edge had been making a cigarette while
Rochford checked the harness tension all
around. Now he struck a match on the rim of
the wagon's nearside wheel, hefted his saddle
and bedroll off the ground to swing it up on to
the footboard, lit the cigarette, dispensed with
the dead match and climbed aboard. Dropped
down on to the seat beside the Englishman and
leaned against the backrest, his legs draped
over his gear.

"You wish me to drive?"

"Your wagon, feller. My mules by default,
but being the kind of animals mules are, they'll
let you know if you don't handle them right."

For the first minutes, Rochford was tentative in the way he used the reins—perhaps as
much because he was aware of being under the
watchful scrutiny of his passenger as from any
self-doubt about his ability to drive the odd
mules and horse team. But then the half-breed
ceased to watch every move the Englishman
made—having seen that he was no novice

driver—and Rochford became comfortably at ease with what he was doing. And his good humor returned to animate his face and put lightness in his voice as he launched into a frank account of his wastrel's progress from the shires of England to every continent of the world and more countries than he could recall. Perhaps unaware that his companion on the seat appeared outwardly to be disinterested in what was being told him—the half-breed's prime concern seeming to be with the no longer flat and open country through which the wagon was rolling.

"Ma'am?" Edge asked in response to the first words Helen Rochford had spoken since she bitingly bawled out her husband before the start from the waterhole.

"The rather crude phrase you used."

"No sweat, ma'am? No trouble is what it means. In understanding what he means right now."

"I rather gather from your general attitude, Mr. Edge—and I have been studying you from in this wagon—that you are completely indifferent to us and everything about us. So I would not expect you to go to any trouble to—"

"Helen, this fellow is our guest and I think you should treat—"

"Don't tell me what I should do or how I should behave, Geoffrey Rochford!" she snarled. "You are in enough trouble with me already. Don't think I've forgotten that you called me stupid and ordered me to be quiet!"

She was speaking very precisely, clearly making an effort to keep her temper—or prevent herself slurring her words.

Edge corrected her: "What he said, ma'am, was for you to shut your stupid mouth. And unless you do that—which still allows you to open it when you have something to say that ain't stupid—you and I will fall out."

"We have never fallen in, mister!" she snapped.

Edge swung around on the seat and pulled the front flap open wider, to peer into the shaded interior of the wagon for the first time. He glimpsed enough of what was in there to form a good general impression of the degree of luxury in which the Rochfords travelled, then concentrated his attention on the woman, who gasped and snatched the glass down from her face as the shaft of sunlight from the opening in the canvas bathed her. She cupped the glass in both slender hands and held it tight into the shallow valley between her meager breasts, as if attempting to conceal it from the glinting eyed gaze of the half breed.

"Geoffrey!" she called weakly.

"No sweat, ma'am," Edge said evenly, allowing the ice coldness of his eyes narrowed to slits to add weight to the threat of what he told her. "You have a pretty mouth. And I'd really hate to mess it up with a fat lip. It wouldn't be polite. So best you just stay quiet in there and keep taking your medicine, uh?"

He jerked the flap closed and turned around

on the seat to face front—but did not confine
his attention to what lay ahead of the slow
rolling wagon. Surveyed, also, the terrain to
either side and every now and then leaned out
to look back the way they had come. For the
five minutes or so it took him to look backwards three times and scan the rest of the landscape perhaps a dozen times, Helen Rochford
maintained a steady monologue of what had
the tone of invective—audible to the men on
the seat but indistinct. While for this same
period, her husband remained tight-lipped and
rigid with tension: offering no clue in his taut
silence to who was the object of his suppressed
anger—himself, his wife or the man beside him.

Then he sucked in some air through his
nostrils and allowed it to be released between
his clenched teeth and just opened lips as a half
hiss-half whistle. And continued to stare
unblinkingly over the backs of the mules and
the horse to the trail they were following as he
said, masking and quickly causing her to cur-
tail her drunken ramblings through the vocab-
ulary of the gutter:

"It will perhaps be better for all concerned,
sir, if we free each other from the bargain we
struck?" His tone seemed to make this a query,
but he went on before Edge could say anything: "Of the two horses we had, the gray
which you so kindly put down for me was the
better animal with a saddle. But I have ridden
the chestnut successfully, while my wife rode
the gray, during a number of side trips. So my

suggestion is that you should take the horse to ride. In exchange for the two mules, which I am sure will get us safely to Tucson in due course. While you will reach your destination far sooner than if you remain with us. Naturally, if you feel such an exchange is not equitable, I shall be happy to make up any reasonable difference with cash money."

Now he shot a brief sideways glance at Edge, his crooked nose face showing an expression that indicated he more than half hoped he would be given an argument.

"Us pay him, you fool?" the woman blurted with a jerky, derisive laugh. "For those two mangy apologies for animals? And do you actually consider he helped us without self interest, Geoffrey? Did you not see the state of his wagon? Why, if he was not riding with us now—as our *guest*, according to you—he would no doubt be attempting to saddle one of his mules, so that he could continue his journey after his wagon became unserviceable."

"Sir, if you try to carry out your threat against my wife, I shall be forced to do what I can to prevent it," Rochford said dully, obviously not eager to get into any kind of fight with the half-breed.

"The mules don't have the mange, feller," Edge said. "Everything else your wife spoke about is true, I guess."

Helen Rochford vented an unladylike grunt of satisfaction in triumph.

"And what I was saying, Edge?" the

Englishman posed, his tone still woeful as he continued to stare morosely along the trail.

"Ain't no denying that it's one of a husband's duties to protect his wife from—"

"I was meaning my suggestion that, if you felt it wise and more convenient for your purpose, you should take the horse and ride on alone?"

It wasn't what he had said at first, and Edge allowed time for the liquored-up woman in the back of the wagon to point this out to her husband. But for several seconds there was just the steady clop of hooves, the chink of harness rings, the creak of moving wagon timbers and the clatter of turning wheel-rims to keep silence out of the arid valley with its bare rock slopes through which the party was headed. Until Edge added the sound of his drawling voice.

"That's my way, feller. Said it back at the place where we met up—like to travel alone. More or less told you awhile back, too, that I wasn't riding the buckboard as a muleteer from choice. But, like I said, your wife was talking some sense just now. The mules ain't sick as such. But the feller who owned them before me didn't take care of them too well. They're old before their time and so they're not up to the kind of heavy work they should be."

"You are saying you think the animals would break if they were asked to pull the wagon without the horse to aid them?" Rochford asked.

"Just listen to the man, Geoffrey," his wife

advised sourly from the back, not sounding so
drunk now: eager for Edge to finish what he
was saying and impatient with her husband for
interrupting.

"You got it, feller. Which means they aren't a
fair exchange for a good, sound horse. Which is
what your gelding is."

"And you don't have the money to cover the
difference?" Helen Rochford said quickly.

"Figure that's my business, ma'am."

"Helen, it is immaterial," Rochford said
grimly. "Since even if Mr. Edge could see his
way clear to paying what he considers Titus to
be worth, we would soon after be in much the
same predicament as we were at the start of
the day."

"Precisely!" his wife said, and there was a
smile in her voice. "I agree. So Edge must remain with us. But not as any guest, Geoffrey.
It seems obvious that he is destitute. So surely
this offers us the opportunity to repay him for
the kindness he has done us in rescuing us from
the Lord knows what terrible fate?"

The redheaded Englishman with the reins
shot a nervous sideways glance at the glinting-
eyed half-breed who shared the seat with him
and asked of the woman behind them: "What
mischief are you hatching now, Helen?"

"Mischief?" she countered in an overstres-
sed tone of injured innocence. "I just have it in
mind to suggest that we pay the man for what
he has done. And will continue to do for us?"

Once more there was a lengthy verbal silence

as the wagon started up a long and gentle slope that veered from west toward south at the head of the low sided valley. This as the sun shifted through the high point of its noontime arc. And the men squinted against the glare, but were not uncomfortably warm—the furnace heat that could be clamped down over this region long gone in the late fall.

Now it was Rochford who waited for Edge to snarl an angry retort—instead of the half-breed allowing the woman time to say something. And, when Edge dug out the makings and began to slowly roll a cigarette, the Englishman found it impossible to wait any longer.

"That is a fine idea, sir! Irrespective of horses and mules, the condition of your wagon and all similar considerations, you should undoubtedly be recompensed for what you are doing for Helen and I. This is your country and we are strangers here. I have seen the way you have constantly remained vigilant. I know you were not boasting when you intimated your ableness with a gun at the moment of our first meeting. And that should you see a threat to us, you will know precisely how to deal with it. Also, you are far more skilled than I in the handling of livestock, Edge. So, what do you say, sir? For as long as it takes us to reach Tucson or some other town where circumstances allow us to part company with safety and amicability, you will act as our guide and mentor, and guard and helper? For an emolument of, let us say, ten shillings a day? I'm sorry—that is two dollars a day. All found, of course."

Edge struck a match on the side of the seat and lit the cigarette, which continued to dangle from a corner of his mouth as he tossed away the dead match and held out both hands to invite the reins.

"What do you say, *Edge?*" Helen Rochford demanded, still emphasising the name so that it was certain not to sound familiar.

"Try never to look a gift horse in the mouth, feller," the half-breed said to the Englishman, who seemed uncertain of why the hands were extended toward him. But now smiled his relief and passed over the reins.

"Very well, then Edge will take over the driving now, Geoffrey," Helen Rochford instructed. "And you will join me here in the wagon, if you please. Come along, hurry up. It is after midday now and time for an *aperitif* before the luncheon stop."

The smile went from Rochford's face, to be replaced by an expression that was a confused mixture of apology, strained patience and entreaty. To which Edge responded with the slightest of shrugs and not an iota of change in the impassive set of his features. Until the Englishman had turned on the seat, swung a leg over the backrest and then dragged his trailing leg after him—to enter the covered rear of the wagon and jerk the flap closed behind him. When he drew back his lips from his teeth to display a smile that failed to inject any warmth into the glinting slivers of his eyes and murmured for his own ears only:

"Have to try now to keep from slugging an old nag in the same place."

Chapter 4

The Rochfords' before-lunch drinking—and rapping—session lasted for over an hour: and would maybe have continued for a lot longer had not Edge located a suitable spot for a stop. At a place a little way off the trail in the fold of two low hills, where an outcrop of rock offered some early afternoon shade and there was a patch of scrub grass on which the animals could graze. And there was adequate kindling and fuel in nearby clumps of brush along the bank of an arroyo to provide a fire.

It was Geoffrey Rochford who built and lit the fire, while his wife prepared and served the meal and the half-breed attended to the needs of the animals.

The meal was cold, served on a folding table spread with a crisp white cover and laid with silver cutlery and china plates, crystal wine glasses and linen napkins. And the only use of the fire was to boil the water with which the woman made tea—that Edge agreed to taste; but after a few sips he placed his own coffeepot among the red embers. He declined a glass of red wine.

During the stop, Geoffrey Rochford was the only member of the trio to show any sign of strain—undertook his share of the chores and then ate his lunch with part of his attention always directed toward his wife or Edge. Obviously concerned that something could happen or be said between them that would trigger a fresh eruption of ill-temper. And, whenever he suspected this was about to take place he was quick to intercede, eagerly allaying trouble before it could get stirred up. The half-breed thought the Englishman had probably drunk too much too fast and had failed to achieve the desired effect of easing the tension he was under.

The man's wife had reached, it seemed to Edge, a plateau of drunkenness on which she gave the impression of being totally in command of everything she did and all she said —provided she concentrated hard. And concentrate she did, to the exclusion of taking account of her husband and the half-breed unless one of them spoke to her or it was absolutely necessary to call their attention to something.

While, for his part, Edge remained as detached as the woman but had no need to work at it. And so felt refreshed by the meal and rested by the pause in the shade of the rock outcrop. Ready to face a long afternoon as driver of the wagon, irrespective of the moods and behavior of the Rochfords—but admitting to himself that his contentment was enhanced by the fact that the English couple elected to ride in the back of the wagon again.

"Helen has to stay out of the sun," Geoffrey Rochford explained in the manner of a man offering an excuse for something that should not have been. "And I'm afraid that I must have eaten something at lunch that disagreed with me."

"No sweat," was all Edge said in reply, with no intonation nor flicker of expression to reveal that he had seen the woman signal to the man that he should join her inside the wagon. For they both had done their share of the chores in breaking the camp.

Neither did he, after the rig had been rolling a few minutes, show to the empty sky, the near barren mountains and the bobbing backs of the three animals in the traces that he could hear the gasps, cries, moans and muted screams of desire and released which were escaping the full-lipped mouth of the blue-eyed, blonde, pale-skinned, slender-bodied woman who was quite obviously sprawled in some attitude of impassioned abandon no more than a dozen feet in back of where he sat.

Sprawled out beneath her husband on the full-size double bed, complete with brass-railed head and foot, that used up such a large part of the wagon's stowage space. Beside the five-section oak chest of drawers with brass handles and the matching wardrobe. And two steamer trunks. A cast iron stove, a half dozen kerosene lamps, several crates of wine and liquor, three chairs, the folding table, a harpsichord, a grandfather clock, cartons containing china and crystal and silverware, a heap of books and two marble statues of rearing horses fashioned to approximately half size scale. The entire freight surely weighing far in excess of the two thousand pounds or so the wagon was designed to carry—and ideally needing four strong draught horses or six good mules to haul it over any kind of terrain that was not flat.

Dammit, they even had four oil paintings on heavy gilt frames hanging from two of the bows. Without revealing anything of what he was thinking, Edge sought to fix his mind on the merely glimpsed subjects of the paintings as Helen Rochford achieved a breathless orgasm and sighed into the weariness of ecstasy. Then, as all became quiet within the wagon behind him and he acknowledged with resignation that he had failed to recall any of the four pictures, the half-breed resumed his vigilant watch over the Gila Mountain landscape.

All his life, it seemed, he had need to be on his guard against the unexpected. As a farm boy in Iowa when, in retrospect, it was always he who sounded the alarm when the bands of hostile Indians approached or a bunch of white no-gooders came by the Hedges place intent upon causing trouble. In truth, it probably had not

been that way at all. His father, his mother and
his kid brother Jamie—even Patch the dog—
had doubtless given the warning as many if not
more times than Josiah C. Hedges. But since
he had become a drifting loner, the man who
was now called Edge found that increasingly
he was recalling the past and its events in
strict terms of how it and they affected him.

After the farmstead there was the War Between the States in which hundreds of thousands of men and women had been caught up.
Josiah C. Hedges had started out as a lieu-
tenant in the Union cavalry, then soon was
promoted to captain. And as such, was always
in command of a troop of men—in particular because of the course his destiny marked out for
him to follow, was in command and close contact with six men whose actions immediately
after the end of the war were to dictate the
pattern of the rest of his life. And yet now, on
this warm afternoon of an Arizona fall day, the
half-breed was able to recall events of the Civil
War only with the backdrops and the other pro-
tagonists blurred and muted while he stood out
in clear and stark isolation at he forefront of
each remembered scene.

It was back then, on the bloodied and scarred
battlegrounds of the east and the south and the
midwest that he had learned to be on his guard
as a practice of habit in order to survive. And
had learned much else, too, which was to stand
him in good stead when he returned to Iowa,
eager to pick up from where he had left off with

his kid brother on the farmstead they had inherited from their peacefully dead parents. But Jamie was dead, too, and his corpse was being torn at by the buzzards on the yard out front of the burned house when Josiah C. Hedges got back home. The men he had commanded—and who were responsible for the brutal murder of Jamie—were not shadowy forms on the far reaches of memory then, when the half-breed went in search of them—using his war-taught skills in the hunt—and in making the kills. Getting his new name of Edge in the process, and stepping across the narrow line to put himself outside the law.

But it was not so much the men of the law he had to keep watch for in the years between the slaking of his thirst for vengeance and a time on the crowded streets of New York City when he was given an amnesty on that old Kansas killing. Then, as now, and out along the many trails that had led from New York City to these Gila Mountains in the Territory of Arizona, the half-breed needed to be on his guard against whatever new threat a malevolent destiny elected to direct at him.

He vented a low grunt of self-annoyance, then busied himself with the rolling of a cigarette as he continued to steer the team along the little used trail at an energy conserving pace. Lit the cigarette and smoked it as he sought to achieve the mood of contentment he had enjoyed at the start of the afternoon drive —before he found it necessary consciously to

blot from his mind the series of images that the
sounds in back of him were capable of conjur-
ing up.

It should not have been this way. He was a
man alone, even in the most crowded of places
—able to remain apart from other people and
oblivious to who they were and what they were
doing, provided they meant him no harm. Yet,
increasingly of late, Edge had found himself
unable to reach that stage of detachment from
his surroundings at which he was dispassionately removed from those of his fellow men
with whom his destiny dictated he should become involved. This, despite the lessons of the
distant past when he had formed attachments,
invariably against his better judgment but
always under a compulsion too powerful to
resist—and been made to suffer in the way that
no man who is truly alone can be punished. For
if a man does what he has to do in order to survive, uncaring of the consequences for others,
and is then able to ride away from the wreck-
age without the need to force any sort of buffer
between himself and the world beyond his own
selfish needs, then surely he is the most complete of men.

Edge took the cigarette from the side of his
mouth, spat at the trail and replaced the cigarette. Glowered toward the dipping sun in the
south-west sky and then became impassive
again. As he decided that those days were
gone. He was younger then, much more resil-
ient and packed full with smartass confidence

in his own ability to fight the world if the world was looking for a fight—and to beat it.

He was still pretty damn confident, although he was not so brash as he used to be. Certainly he was not so young. And, maybe, he was lacking in resilience nowadays. Being a drifting loner was a life for a man of fewer years than . . .

"The hell with that!" the half-breed rasped through clenched teeth abruptly bared between drawn back lips, the sentiment barely audible to his own ears. Why did he always have to search for an explanation about his thought processes at times when images he had not consciously called upon began to sneak into his mind?

Helen Rochford was not his kind of woman, but she was a fine looker and she was the first woman he had clapped eyes on since he left the town of Calendar a lot of days before. He had needed to kill a woman in that town. A woman who . . . he forced himself to abandon that line of thought and was satisfied he had good reason for this. Just as there was a good reason why, as a man in the present circumstances, he should have experienced a vicarious pleasure tinged with more than a little envy, when he heard the wife being taken by her husband almost within touching distance of where he sat.

"Mr. Edge!" Geoffrey Rochford said suddenly, as he jerked open the front flap of the wagon canvas. And the half breed felt another stab of self-annoyance—that he had failed to be

aware of stirrings within the wagon. But then,
as he dropped the tiny butt of the cigarette to
the trail, he ridded himself of this feeling, too.
If a new danger was hovering just out of range
of his sensory perception, the Englishman was
not it. And during the period of introspection
that Rochford had interrupted, Edge had maintained his constant surveillance over the
barren and arid mountain country through
which he was driving the wagon.

"Yeah, feller?"

"Helen and I usually pause for tea at about
four each afternoon."

The Englishman was minus his hat, his red
hair was tousled, his green eyes had the grit of
sleep in them and his tanned skin looked a little
puffy. Then the gap in the canvas was abruptly
made wider and his wife appeared at his side,
looking more dishevelled than him from the
liquor and bed. She had taken off more than
just her hat, but was careful not to reveal anything other than the paleness of one shoulder
as she clutched a blanket together with both
hands at her throat.

"Figure it's way past five now," Edge
answered after a brief glance at the couple who
squinted in the sunlight.

"Six even, do you think?" the woman asked,
sounding brighter than she looked.

"Not far off it, ma'am."

"Then we shall not bother with tea. At six,
we always halt to make camp. Then have a
before-dinner *aperitif.* Kindly be on the look-

out for a suitable place to stop while I get dressed."

She withdrew into the rear of the wagon as her husband fished a watch from a pocket of his vest and then had difficulty in bringing the face into focus.

"You know, it is fifteen minutes to six o'clock, Mr. Edge," he said, impressed. He replaced the watch with the precise actions of a drunken man determined to do it right. "And I think the only timepiece you have is the sun, is that not correct?"

"Never known the sun to gain or lose," Edge answered, and glanced again at Rochford: realized the Englishman was a good deal drunker than he looked.

"Geoffrey!" his wife called.

"You know what I mean."

"Yeah, I know."

"Ah, but what do you do on dull days, sir? When the sky is clouded over?"

"On those days, neither the sun nor me are so hot."

"Geoffrey, come help me with the fastenings on this dress!" Helen Rochford demanded sharply. "And allow the driver to attend to the task I have given him!"

The Englishman ducked back into the rear of the wagon. And the half-breed remained impassive, the set of his features an honest representation of his lack of inner reaction to the woman's imperious scorn. Some ten minutes later he tugged on the reins to steer the team

off the trail as it emerged from a narrow ravine,
to halt the rig at the base of a fifty-foot-high
bluff where some scrub grass, brush and
stunted cottonwood grew. A place where the
animals had a little spartan forage to graze on
and which would provide shelter in the event of
a sudden norther blowing up. In other respects
offered little as a campsite, but then the Rochfords were equipped to make the best of the
most spartan surroundings. And within an
hour of the wagon rolling to a halt, the area between the rig and the face of the cliff, the hobbled animals and the cottonwoods was like a
cozy parlor which lacked only the walls, the
ceiling and a stove to contain the fire. Then, a
little later, when night settled over the Gila
Mountains, it was easier still to experience an
eerie sense of unreality—when the kerosene
lamps were lit to dim the moon and black out
the world beyond the limits of their fringe
glow. While within the confines set by the light
of the lamps and the fire, there was spread
much of the clutter from the wagon—the table
and the two chairs, the chest of drawers with
some of the china ornaments on its top, the
harpsichord, the grandfather clock which had
been put right and started, and even a rug that
was unrolled on the ground between the fire
and the table.

Thus, the chores in setting up the night camp
were more numerous than those when the
lunch stop was made, and the Rochfords were
sobered by the work involved. Even though

they each sipped at a whisky from time to time. Edge did no more at this camp than at the earlier one and was aware as he did what was necessary that the Englishman became tense again while the woman's mood was one of contentment on the brink of excitement. Sometimes she even hummed tunelessly, which served to heighten her husband's obvious foreboding.

The meal was a beef stew with sweet potatoes and there was red wine to go with it. And there was brandy to go with or into the coffee after the food was eaten. The Rochfords had all of this, and then had several refills of the brandy into their crystal balloons after the woman had moved her chair from the table to the harpsichord which she could play more melodiously than she could hum.

For his part, the half-breed ate the meal and drank two cups of coffee: passed on the wine and the brandy. Just as at lunch time, he sat at the table on his saddle. After this meal, he dragged his saddle closer to the base of the bluff and used it as a pillow when his bedroll was unfurled and he slid under the blankets—sharing the cover with his Winchester rifle.

He had removed only his gunbelt, which he draped over the horn of the saddle: and his hat which he placed over his face to blot out the fire and lamplight. There was no way by which he could cut himself off from the music, but it had, in combination with some languid thoughts, a pleasing soporific effect on him—to an extent

where he was unaware of when Helen Rochford
stopped playing the instrument, and heard
nothing of what occurred between his final
conscious reflection and the time when a hand
gently shook his shoulder and she asked with
deep feeling:

"You didn't mean what you said, did you?"

As always happened, Edge came awake to in-
stant total recall. Knew it was still night because of the darkness under his hat—and that
the meager light which did get in below the
brim to tease his eyes was from the dying fire.
The lamps had been turned out. He knew, also,
from her tone of voice that the woman was
drunk.

"What did I say that I didn't mean, ma'am?"
he asked, using both hands to lift his hat off his
face, then place it on his head as he folded up
into a sitting position.

"When you said you didn't like me."

She remained kneeling at his side, her hands
gripping her thighs which, like the rest of her
from ankle and wrist to throat were enveloped
in a nightgown that looked to be made of many
layers of diaphanous fabric that in a lesser
quantity would be both revealing and clinging.

Her husband was nowhere to be seen in the
merest of glimmers from the embers of the fire
—the moon was hidden behind cloud that completely blanketed the sky. But the English-
mans' presence in the bed aboard the wagon
was signalled by the regular sounds of his
whistling snores. Briefly, Rochford's snoring

was in competition with the grandfather clock as it chimed the hour of three in the morning.

"Well, I'll tell you, Mrs. Rochford," Edge said as the final chime receded out along the valleys and curled over the ridges of the surrounding mountains. "I figure you have to be one of the worst bitches the Lord ever created."

She gasped her mouth wide and it and her eyes were the sole areas of darkness about her from head to toe, for her skin was as pale as the white nightgown. But instead of the shrieked abuse he expected, Helen Rochford laughed— softly and not for long.

"That all?" the half-breed asked.

"Meaning?"

"You woke me up to ask me a question. My answer gave you a laugh. All right for me to go back to sleep now?"

"You expected me to do anything but laugh, I think?"

"Understanding women is something I've decided to give up trying to do, ma'am."

She nodded, the smile that had spread across her pale and beautiful face in the wake of the terse laugh becoming more firmly set. "I do not wish to be understood as a woman, Edge. Just to be made to feel like one."

Slowly, she moved her hands up from her thighs to her throat. Without shifting them away from the frothy fabric of what she wore— her actions unsubtly erotic as her pale fingers trailed up and over her body. To locate the tie

fastening at the neckline of the garment.
Which she suddenly released, then shrugged
her shoulders and spread wide her arms. And
the nightgown was seen to be more like a coat
than a dress, without any fastening except at
the neck. So that the woman was at once naked
at the front from her throat to where her knees
were on the ground. Her slender body as pale
as her face, except for the darkened areas on
the crests of her small breasts and the not quite
so pronounced triangular patch at the base of
her belly.

"I think you understand this, *Edge?*" she
said breathlessly, stressing that she was calling him by his surname again.

"Ain't hard, Mrs. Rochford."

"So you know what is required of you. As a
hired man, you have to do as I tell you and I am
telling you to get out from under those blankets and—"

"Like I just told you, lady, it ain't hard," the
half-breed cut in, needing to consciously force
something akin to a natural tone into his voice
as her nakedness stirred his sexuality.

"Laughing time is over, mister! I need a man
and since you're the only—"

Despite all else that was happening, Edge
heard when Rochford ceased snoring. When he
was midway through drawling:

"If that's the case, best you cover yourself
up and go back to bed. On account of I've seen
women got bigger nipples than you've got tits.
And as for that beaver, I figure a mouse—"

"You bastard!" the woman screamed, and slammed her arms down to her sides so that the nightgown floated gently in at either side to envelop her again. But before it did, and while the half-breed had switched his narrow-eyed gaze to the rear of the wagon, Helen Rochford's arms moved again. And she rose up on her knees as she leaned forward.

"Helen!" Geoffrey Rochford yelled, horror etched deeply into his face and injecting shrillness into his voice as he started down the steps that reached from the rear of the wagon to the ground.

Edge had glimpsed, on the periphery of his vision while he looked toward the wagon, the sudden moves of the woman. Then realized she was reaching for the Colt in the holster of the gunbelt draped over the saddlehorn. But was too late to prevent her getting a double-handed grip on the butt. Had time only to whirl toward her on his rump, letting go of the blankets he had been about to slide beneath again. His hands streaking toward hers and closing over them as she thumbed back the hammer and pushed the forefingers of both hands through the triggerguard.

"No, Helen, no!" her husband screamed.

"Die, you bastard!" the woman rasped.

Edge could not tear the revolver out of her grasp. Could only, by brute strength allied with the determination to survive, wrench her hands and arms and upper body to the side—this against the woman's enraged determination to kill him which seemed to imbue her with a power out of proportion to her slight physique.

The gun cracked and the woman gasped as she stared at it: like she was shocked by the fact of it firing. Then she coughed against the acrid attack of the black powder smoke in her throat. A moment later screamed as she stared fixedly across the bizarrely equipped night camp, and ceased to fight the half-breed's tacit demand for the Colt.

And now Edge looked in the same direction she did as he plucked the revolver easily out of her hands. Was in time to see Geoffrey Rochford, blood oozing from his forehead and down his broken nose, pitch backwards off the steps and sprawl out, arms to the sides and legs splayed, on the ground at the rear of the wagon.

"Dear God!" Helen Rochford moaned, covering her face with her hands as she struggled to her feet. "What have I done? Geoffrey! Have I killed my husband?"

"If you haven't, lady," Edge said evenly as he came erect and pushed the Colt into the waistband of his pants at his belly, "no one can say you didn't have a pretty good shot at it."

Chapter Five

Edge heard running footfalls and labored breathing behind him as he went around the fire, between the table and the harpsichord. But did not glance toward the woman until he reached the gunshot man and dropped to his haunches beside Geoffrey Rochford. For the sounds made by the barefoot woman in the flimsy nightgown were receding. So she meant him no harm. And then she began to wail her horror at the harm she had already done, just as the half-breed cupped his hands to his mouth to form a bullhorn and yell:

"Your husband ain't dead, lady!"

He guessed that she heard his voice against the shrill, animalistic sound venting from her own lips but perhaps was not able to understand the words he said. Or expected the worst and so purposely misheard him. Whichever, she kept on running—out on to the trail and southward along it. Still visible as a wraithlike form in the billowing garment for some time after the frenetic sounds of her panicked retreat had faded from earshot.

But, eventually, as Edge prodded the embers
of the fire into bright flames and set a skillet of
water to boiling, he glanced for a final time
after the Englishwoman and failed to glimpse
her. Then devoted his entire attention to what
had to be done for the injured man. Which
seemed little enough at first: for Rochford,
although he was unconscious, looked to Edge
to have suffered only a minor flesh wound. The
bullet from the handgun having inscribed a
long wound across his forehead, shallow where
it began above the right eye and where it ended
above the left: but perhaps bone deep above
the bridge of the nose. So it was more likely the
fall to the ground, maybe after he tripped on
the hem of his long nightshirt, that had
plunged the man into unconsciousness, rather
than the effect of the bullet that had done little
more than graze him—with fast decaying
velocity after traveling so many feet across the
camp.

But the half-breed, inwardly cursing behind
his impassive facade this fresh trouble, treated
Geoffrey Rochford where he lay—just in case
moving the senseless man might create a dangerous side effect to his condition. A treatment
that was not complex, carried out in the bright
light of two kerosene lamps placed on the steps
at the rear of the wagon. First Edge bathed the
three-inch length of the gory wound with boiled
water that had cooled a little and then he dried
it, spread some antiseptic salve on it and lay a
strip of clean, white fabric over it: the salve

taken from a medicine box he found in the wardrobe aboard the wagon while the temporary dressing and the pieces of rag he had used to clean and dry the wound were torn from one of Helen Rochford's cotton chemises he took from the chest of drawers.

After this was done, he doused both the lamps, went to the fire, stirred new flames from its embers and sat on the one chair that was still at the table. The bottle of brandy, almost half full, was on the table and he took a drink from its neck. Then poured a generous measure into one of the two crystal balloons that flanked the bottle. Made a cigarette and lit it before he sipped at the brandy. Gazed pensively southward along the trail but could not see very far on this moonless night: saw not a sign of the woman in white. Then, the cigarette not a quarter smoked and the brandy sipped at only twice, he shifted his attention toward Rochford as the clock chimed once to mark three thirty and the injured man called:

"Helen?"

He sounded fully conscious and miserably aware of what had happened to him. But he continued to be sprawled in the same attitude with his arms spread wide and his legs splayed, like he was staked out.

"You're stuck with me, feller," the half-breed answered as he rose from the chair, carrying the brandy balloon.

"Edge?" Rochford's head seemed as transfixed as his body and limbs. "She didn't kill you? My God, what an awful mess. You didn't shoot . . .?''

"I figure she thinks she killed you, feller," the half-breed answered as he came to a halt beside the spread-eagled man and realized the bullet had done more than merely crease Rochford's flesh. "Took off into the night. You can't see, can you?"

"That's what makes it so awful," the Englishman answered in a dull tone as his eyes continued to remain unmoving at the centers of their sockets, staring sightlessly up at the cloud blanketed darkness of the sky from between unblinking lids. "I thought at first the dressing was over my eyes but it isn't, is it?"

"No."

"It didn't touch my eyes, did it? The bullet?"

"No. Didn't do anything but take out a strip of your skin, feller. On the outside."

"It could merely be a temporary condition. I must hope that is so, anyway. But meantime, Helen is my prime concern, sir. She was almost . . . she had on . . . she was insufficiently attired for roaming about at night. And that apart, this country is not the ideal place for a woman alone to—"

"Sure, we'll go look for her," Edge cut in after he had taken the contents of the brandy balloon at a single swallow and as he hung the cigarette back at the side of his mouth. "Just as soon as you feel able to travel."

"Which is now, sir," the Englishman answered at once and, well practiced in the matter of taking care to seem to do things with dignity when he was drunk, he got stiffly to his feet despite being blind, groggy and in no little pain. But then had to request: "I fear it will be necessary for me to ride in the rear, Mr. Edge? And I do not . . ."

He extended both arms and shuffled around in a half turn. Then brought one hand back to his face, to hold the loose dressing in place over the bullet wound.

"No sweat, feller," the half-breed told him, took hold of the wrist of his extended arm and turned the man, to lead him to the rear of the wagon and place his free hand on a strut of the steps. "Can you make it inside while I fix the team?"

"Thank you, yes. And thank you so much for what you have already done for me. While I was even less able to fend for myself."

"No sweat."

Edge remained at the rear of the wagon, close enough to reach out and support Geoffrey Rochford if he slipped. But then, when the Englishman was safely aboard, he moved away to break camp. First buckled on his gunbelt and replaced the revolver in the holster. Next gathered up his gear and stowed it on the footboard of the wagon—kept out of his bedroll just a sheepskin coat which he donned against the chill of the night after he had put the two mules and the horse into the traces and doused the fire. Finally rummaged quickly through the contents of the chest of drawers to ensure the

Rochfords kept nothing valuable in among the
clothing, then stowed the steps and raised the
tailgate of the wagon. Said as he completed
this:

"There's nothing I'm leaving here that's
needed to help locate your wife, feller."

"I ask nothing else but that you find Helen
for me, sir," the man in the bed answered morosely. "And, of course, in view of the additional
inconvenience you have been put to on our behalf, there will be an adjustment in the remun-
eration you will receive."

Edge moved along the side of the wagon and
climbed up on to the seat. Spoke a quiet word
of command to the animals and flicked the
reins as he released the brake lever. Then, back
on the trail, he held the reins between his knees
while he slid the Colt from the holster, extracted the expended shell case and pushed a
fresh round into the chamber. Said over his
shoulder as he thrust the revolver back into the
holster:

"Long as she heads down the trail to Tucson,
it's no inconvenience to me."

He thought the injured man had failed to
hear him, but it was unimportant and so he did
not repeat himself. And perhaps as long as a
half minute had elapsed when the Englishman
replied:

"My wife attempted to kill you."

"She made a lousy job of it."

"You have not agreed so readily to help me

find her so that you may pay her back for that?"

Edge spat off the side of the wagon and rasped: "I don't give a shit about your wife, feller. Which means as far as I'm concerned, she ain't worth taking the time to repay. By smacking her in the mouth, paddling her butt or squeezing a trigger. I'm going to Tucson and if I happen to spot your wife on the way, I'll let you know. If ain't much, but I guess the way things are for you, it's the kindest—"

"There is something you should know about me that will explain the situation between Helen and I, Mr. Edge. And explain, too, why she was driven to act in such a wanton manner tonight."

"I just got through telling you it doesn't matter to me what—"

"I am impotent, Mr. Edge. Married to a woman with perhaps more than the average needs in that direction. Able to do no more than give Helen a poor substitute for the fulfillment she so desperately desires. A beautiful woman, as you must agree, Mr. Edge? Sexually attractive to every normal man who sees her. And I mean normal in the sense of being capable of offering her fulfillment, sir.

"Until now—until tonight—she has always been able to resist temptation, Mr. Edge. It has been sheer hell for her and for me. You have seen how we drink too much. Heard how she treats me like dirt when the mood takes her.

But a man such as I must indulge a woman such as she, sir. She is beautiful and I am proud to be married to her—to have her for my own even though I can never possess her the way other men possess their women."

"None of this is my business, feller," the half-breed said when Rochford paused, perhaps to compose himself so that he could stem the tears that were threatening to spill from his sightless eyes.

"I want you to know. So that you will not think so harshly of Helen. Will you continue to listen to me, please?"

From far to the west came the call of a coyote, too subdued by distance to disturb the trio of animals in the traces of the wagon so that the constantly rhythmic sounds of the easy-moving rig continued without interruption.

"I've always been a better listener than a talker, feller," Edge said.

"Have you ever been married or had a woman—"

"I was married, but that ain't the reason I'm a better listener than a—"

"If you can make jokes about the woman you loved then you never loved her as much as—"

"It's your wife you want to talk about!" the half-breed cut in, and his voice was as cold as the glint in the narrowed eyes that gazed momentarily back through the years.

But then Edge forced his mind to the present. And was in time to hear the man in the

back of the wagon vent a gasp of fear. Before
Rochford said, as the half-breed took up his
raking survey of the night-draped Gila Mountains:

"I'm sorry. I was wrong about you, sir. It
was recently you lost your wife. It was because
of the memory of her you responded to the advances of my wife the way you did?"

"It was a long time ago, feller, and my wife
has nothing to do with anything about you or
your wife. You want the truth, I could have
screwed your wife without needing to think
about it. If you hadn't been around. Which was
before I knew the way you were and while she
was showing me what was available. You know
what I mean? I told you I listened better than I
talked."

"You're a liar, Mr. Edge."

"Your opinion, feller."

"Not as regards your ability to listen as opposed to talking," Geoffrey Rochford countered, a little impatiently. "As well as you know.
You are not the kind of man who could have
possessed any woman who approached you in
the manner that Helen did. I am afraid that
Helen has been married to a man without balls
—if you understand my meaning—for so long
that she must metaphorically castrate every
man with whom she comes into contact.

"It has happened time and time again in the
past. Every man she has come into contact
with has been made to look small—or else she
will have nothing to do with him. From hotel

bellboy up to my friends, some of whom are the cream of English aristocracy, sir. In such instances, she is humored or my money serves to smooth ruffled pride. But, dear God, when I heard what was happening at the encampment tonight, I thought that perhaps I had driven Helen insane. That such a beautiful and desirable woman should seek to dominate a man into taking her—and a man such as you. When her common sense should have warned her that you, being the kind of man you are, would be antagonized by such a—"

Rochford abruptly curtailed what he was saying, like somebody who had been killing time with talk until he heard something he was waiting for. Or maybe . . .

"You in trouble, feller?" Edge asked, hopeful of the opposite—that the helpless Englishman fate had forced into his care had begun to get his sight back.

But it was not to be. "All you appear to be doing, sir, is driving this wagon along the trail at the same speed as before," Rochford announced suspiciously.

"We didn't leave too much behind, feller," Edge answered. "And the animals didn't have a full night at—"

"I am not criticizing you on that score, sir. It is still night?"

"Getting close to four in the morning. Guessing that from the time by the clock when we left—"

"No moon still?"

"Right."

"So you are making no attempt to track Helen?"

Edge held the reins between his knees again, this time while his hands were busy with taking out the makings and rolling a cigarette.

"I told you, feller. Tucson is where I'm headed. And if she's on the trail still, there's a good chance we'll catch up with her."

"But what if she wandered off the trail?"

"Barefoot and the night as dark as it is, I figure it would take the best Indian tracker moving at a snail's pace to pick up her sign and follow it."

Rochford took some time to think this over and once more the coyote in the far distance of the west vented a howl, the call hardly audible above the noise of the moving wagon and the animals which hauled it.

"Perhaps I should ride on the seat with you?"

"You should?"

"Perhaps she may go into hiding when she hears our approach. If she sees you alone, she will fear the worst. But if I am in view . . .?"

"Could you make it out here, sitting up, for very long, feller?"

"I don't know, Mr. Edge. No, you are probably right."

"Try if you want. But if you keel over and fall off the wagon, I'm not going to doctor you again."

"God, what a mess!"

"If it helps any, I think she'll have enough sense to stay close to the trail. After she got over the jolt of what she thought she'd done to you. And I figure, too, that when she sees the wagon she'll risk me blasting her to hell instead of facing up to much longer running around these mountains with next to nothing on."

The silence from behind the half-breed was considerably longer than before and he kept an open mind about the reason for this as he smoked his cigarette and maintained his watch over the unspectacular hills on all sides.

Then Geoffrey Rochford said dully: "You know, I think you're right. She'll be sober by now and she has a lot of sense when she's sober."

"So you can quit worrying about her, feller. And let go about yourself, uh? No better place to keel over than in bed when there's nowhere to fall."

The Englishman vented a strangled cry that became a sob. And managed to choke out before his stored up misery was released in full flood: "Dear God, you certainly can see through people!"

To which Edge answered evenly: "Well, I ain't blind."

Chapter Six

The Englishman took a long time to expend his grief and misery at being blind. Or maybe it wasn't long at all for a man to come to terms with such a disability. Edge allowed, as he watched the dawn of a new day break. A day that gave early promise of being grey and sunless, but would still be a whole lot better to see than to be blind to.

"God, I'm sorry, Mr. Edge," Rochford said after several minutes had passed since his final, body-shuddering sob.

"No sweat."

"Thank you for understanding. A man like you must find that difficult to do."

"Maybe a man that never cried is less of a man because of it, feller."

"Your wife made you weep, Mr. Edge?"

"Losing her did. And speaking of wives, we've just found yours."

"Is she . . . ?"

Geoffrey Rochford sounded emotionally drained and physically exhausted as he spoke the query in a rasping whisper from the cov-

ered rear of the wagon. And Helen Rochford
looked to be in a similar state of near collapse.

Since the light of breaking dawn had first
started to drive back the darkness of night,
Edge had paid particular attention to a stand
of timber that was some three miles distant
when he first saw it. Did not entirely ignore the
terrain to either side of and behind the slow,
quietly rolling wagon but was unable to rid
himself of a conviction that if he and his blond
charge were not alone in this mountainscape,
company waited in the trees. Which was an in-
tuitive impression he would have given no cre-
dence to had not the flanking country and that
behind been an expanse of rolling hills of soft
rock eroded by weather to a series of smooth,
almost featureless slopes among which no one
who posed a threat could be concealed at close
quarters to the trail. Maybe the woman was
out there in the hills, but she alone was no
danger. Whereas every enemy the half-breed
had ever made and allowed to live could have,
with ease, been hidden among the pinion and
brush into which the trail plunged after running through these near-barren southwest foot-
hills of the Gila Mountains. And so it was that
Edge looked more often at the trees than elsewhere, his right hand ready to move fast to
where the stock of the Winchester jutted out of
the boot on the saddle against which he rested
his leg. But he felt unfamiliarly uneasy as,
while he talked with Rochford, he saw the
Englishman's wife appear on the trail—and

had to admit to himself that his intuition had been right.

"She's on her feet, feller. She's looked a whole lot better, but I'd guess your wife's in finer shape than you are."

He was seeing the woman over a distance of some three hundred yards when he told this to Rochford, she having emerged from the timber to the right and moved out of the stand to halt on the center of the open trail, emphatic in her determination to stop the rig or else be run down by it.

She was totally naked and made not even a token attempt to cover any part of herself with her hands and arms that hung loosely at her sides. She had moved in an awkward gait, a stiff-legged stagger, and when she came to a halt she planted her feet firmly on the ground and swayed for several moments before she was able to hold still. Many of what at first appeared to be dirt smudges on the pale skin of her body were seen as the wagon closed with her to be bruises, ugly dark in hue: on her breasts and shoulders, her thighs and belly. Her face was unmarked by physical abuse, but there were areas of darkness beneath her blue eyes that were red-rimmed, and her cheeks looked hollower, her mouth almost lipless in a leaden mask molded by a harrowing experience with evil. Her honey-colored hair was tangled and matted, caught with the debris of a forest floor.

Even as he hauled on the reins to bring the

wagon to a halt, the dipped head of the chestnut gelding just six feet from where the naked
woman stood, Edge continued to distrust the
brush thickened timber behind her; he remained tensed to slide the rifle from the boot at
the first sign that Helen Rochford was an en-
forced part of an ambush.

"Whatever you do to me, it will be nothing
compared to—" the Englishwoman began in a
tone even more lackluster than the expression
on her gaunt face, looking across the animals
and up at the half-breed in a fixed stare not un-
like that he had seen in the sightless eyes of her
husband peering uselessly up at the night sky.
But then she saw movement at the same moment Edge heard it, and incredulity abruptly
showed through the hopelessness and exhaustion in her blue eyes when they shifted direction, and she cried, "Geoffrey? Geoffrey . . . oh
dear God in heaven . . ."

"Helen! Helen, my darling! Come to me,
please!"

"I thought I'd—"

"And I thought we would never—"

She started around from the front to the side
of the animals in the traces, as Edge leaned out
to look back at where her husband was feeling
his way forward—one hand on the wheel and
then the timbers of the wagon while the other
was outstretched, eager for the first contact
with his wife.

"You're blind, Geoffrey?" she almost
screamed, and glanced up at Edge.

"Like love is, they say, lady," the half-breed murmured, but was not heard as Helen Rochford quickened her pace and flung her arms about her husband.

She sobbed and struggled to babble out a tearful explanation in answer to his tremulously voiced questions about her nakedness, her presence so far from the night camp and what she had first said to the half-breed when the wagon came to a stop. Edge heard only the first few stumbling queries and hardly any of what the woman started to reply—then nothing at all after he had climbed down off the wagon and moved, Winchester canted to his shoulder, along the trail and into the trees. Where he found the spot in the brush Helen Rochford had been before she moved out into the open when the wagon approached. Nothing bad had happened to her here, and there was no layer of loose dust on the hard packed dirt of the trail to hold impressions of her bare feet and show in which direction she had come to get here. But maybe she had stumbled between the trees through the brush. Edge did not consider it worthwhile checking this out. For he was merely killing time beyond earshot of the husband and wife until they were through with what they had to say to each other, and going through the motions of making sure the man— or men—who attacked her were not nearby.

Abruptly he sighed with a sound that had the tone of a low curse, and leaned the rifle against a tree trunk as he sat on a prominent

root and took the makings from his shirt
pocket. Turned the collar of the sheepskin coat
up around his neck against the chill of the
morning air once the cigarette was lit. Going
through the motions of doing anything for the
benefit of other people's sensibilities was something else that was not characteristic of him.
The sooner they reached Tucson and he could
part company with the Rochfords the better.
Favor repaid with favor and nobody owning a
part of anybody else. Except for the husband
and the wife, of course, but that was nothing to
do with—

"Edge!"

The cigarette was smoked down to the smallest of butts when this calling of his name
jerked the half-breed out of another morose
reverie: and he dropped it to the grass and
stepped on it as he rose from the tree root,
scooping up the Winchester to cant it to his
shoulder. His face, thickly covered with more
than twenty-four hours of grey and black
bristles, was in its usual impassive set. But
perhaps the glint in the slitted eyes beneath
the hooded lids was a fraction icier than was
usual—in response to the way Geoffrey Rochford had snarled his name. In the same tone his
wife had often used, but yelled much louder
than she ever did—to imply a command from a
man in authority to one of lesser rank.

"Edge, can you hear me!" the Englishman
demanded with even more impatient insistence
as the half-breed stepped out of the pinion and

halted on the same spot where the woman had waited. The woman who now, her nakedness enveloped in an all-black dress, came from around the rear of the wagon, finger-combing pine needles and dead leaves from her hair until she caught hold of her husband's arm to shake it and rasp anxiously:

"Geoffrey, he's here!"

"Four of them, Edge! One of them a Negro! Bearded and stinking from not washing! All of them wearing coats to their ankles that were once white! Each of them with a horse! You'll take Titus and go after them, Edge! And you'll kill them! Then bring back their coats to show to Helen! So she'll know you've killed them!"

He stared in frantic blindness from side to side, head cocked to the side to listen for Edge to make a move and both arms outstretched to touch him.

"I will, feller?" the half-breed posed evenly.

"I will pay one thousand dollars per coat, sir!" Rochford vowed, his head still and his arms down at his sides.

The tall, slightly built Englishman was still dressed only in his nightshirt, which was something Edge had not taken note of until now. For earlier, when Rochford had appeared at the side of the wagon eager to hold his wife and on this occasion when he needed more desperately to buy vengeance against the men who violated her, the powerful intensity of his bullet-scarred and blind-eyed face caused everything else about him to withdraw into out-of-focus insignificance. Until, as he waited for the half-breed to reply, he feared a refusal. And realized that if this came, he was totally helpless in such a situation as he found himself. So the demanding demeanor was suddenly gone from his face, to be replaced by an expression of pathos, the extent of which was deepened and broadened by the man's unsuitable clothing on this dull-skied, cold-aired morning. Just as another contribution was made by the way in which Rochford cocked his head to one side again, in the listening attitude of a dumb animal anxious for the reward of a kind word for a task done.

"Please, Mr. Edge," the misused woman asked, her voice husky with controlled emotion. "I know I have no right to ask the smallest favor of you. But after what I have done to poor Geoffrey . . . ?"

"I don't kill people for money, feller." Edge said.

"Then capture them and bring them to the justice of the law!" Rochford said quickly, encouraged that he had received a qualified response from the half-breed. And needing to work at keeping in check a natural urge to become domineering again.

"No!" his wife exclaimed, and of a sudden there was bitter vindictiveness in her tone, her face and even the way her body became rigid.

"Helen?" her husband asked, puzzled, turning his head to look blindly back at her.

"I wish to be certain they pay with their lives for what they did to me," she replied to the questioner but stared at Edge. "So capture the scum and bring them to me, Mr. Edge. So that I may put them down like the animals they are. If you cannot deal with them in such a way yourself."

"Helen, you don't know what you're saying!" Rochford warned, shocked now as he turned to face the half-breed as if he hoped Edge would support him. While his wife stood to the side and slightly behind him, looking capable of committing far greater carnage than the gunning down of the four men who raped her.

And it was easy for Edge to think, as she stared fixedly at him, that she was contemplating a much worse fate for him should he side with her husband and refuse the new deal.

"Four thousand dollars," she urged. "Merely for rounding them up and bringing them in, Mr. Edge—to use one of your western expressions. And I will attend to the slaughtering myself. Make you perhaps the most highly paid hired hand who ever rode—"

"Helen, we are both overwrought now," Rochford put in anxiously, struggling to regain his composure. "It is only natural after what has happened to you. But it is not cattle you are speaking of and when they—"

There was a smile of malevolent evil on the gaunt face of the woman as she said with slow, soft spoken sincerity: "No, my dear. I feel it . . . I know . . . that as time passes, my resolve to kill those animals will only harden."

"Edge, explain to her that these men will—"

"I only ever worked but once in the cattle business, lady," the half-breed said across Rochford's plea. "Even that time, I had more dealings with the men than the steers. So I don't figure I'll have much trouble in rounding up and bringing in four cowpokes."

Chapter Seven

If the distraught Helen Rochford had not mis-heard the talk among the men and they did not alter their plans, the task of finding the quartet of rapists was not going to be difficult. But as he rode into the timber, away from the stalled wagon beside which the English couple were fixing a fire on which to boil water for their morning tea, Edge made no presumptions. At first attended to the reaching of an understand-ing between himself and the chestnut gelding which was not supposed to be the best riding horse in the southwest. Then, after this rapport was established, he spent some more time in relishing for its own sake the sense of freedom that came with being alone again. And not only this—being alone astride his own saddle cinched to the back of a horse. A horse that would have been fine even if he was the meanest sonofabitch that was ever broken-in—to a man who seemed to have spent half a life-time on a buckboard and then a covered wagon.

Not so long, really. Just since a lusting Frenchman who operated a ferryboat shot his

last mount. The object of the ferryman's lust
was a young Arapaho girl who . . . But that was
all in the past and the past should be left in
peace unless there were lessons to be learned
from it. Or good times to be recalled, maybe.
And there was nothing good to be reflected
upon between the time he found Nalin after the
brutal slaughter of so many of her people, and
this gray morning when he rode away from the
wagon. Just the one lesson, perhaps, which it
seemed he was incapable of learning—that if he
truly desired total freedom, he should avoid
every last one of his fellowmen like each of
them was infected with the bubonic plague.
And ride the widest swing around those who
were in trouble.

But a man had to eat and to feed his horse,
needed to clothe himself and replace his gear
from time to time. And in this country where
the frontiers of civilization and the conventions
it brought with it closed tighter around a man
with each passing day—or so it seemed—he
needed to have money in his pocket to pay his
way. Unless he was a thief, needed to earn the
money. As he was doing now—the bidding of
another man, and so was unable to enjoy the
brand of consummate satisfaction that came
only with total freedom. That had not been his
lot since the pall of smoke against a bright blue
sky signalled the end of his lone ride from Wy-
oming to the border of the Indian Country with
New Mexico Territory and he found Nalin . . .

He reached the fork in the trail of which

Helen Rochford had spoken and reined in his new mount: dismissed from his mind all thoughts of what once might have been to devote his entire attention to what was necessary now as he swung down from the saddle to look closely at the trail. At the point where it reached a towering pinnacle of granite and divided into two, heading southeast and southwest. In the densest section of the timber he had ridden through since he entered the forest perhaps a mile and a half to the north.

This was where the woman had been forced to suffer her ordeal of repeated rape by the four men who were camped on the grassy area at the base of the rearing crag in the fork of the trails. It was a long time since she had run away from the other camp under another bluff in the hill country, she said. But it seemed a long time, too, before the wagon came into sight at the beginning of the day. She had no thought of ever seeing the wagon and its driver again, though, while she made her exhausted and shivering way out of the hills and into the timber. Maddened by grief because she was certain she had killed her husband. And terrified that Edge would seek her out and punish her for trying to kill him.

She was on the verge of collapse when she saw the glimmer of firelight through the trees. But was disorientated and hysterical. For a second she was sure she had doubled back on herself in the darkness, to stagger toward instead of away from the place where her hus-

band lay dead and a stranger prepared to kill
her. And despair became mixed in with the
other powerful emotions that had served to
keep her running through the night. Caused
something to snap in her mind so that, just for
a moment, she was deranged—and she began
to scream. Another moment later, sanity returned and she realized that escape to safety
depended upon silence: at the same time became aware she was in the forest instead of
among barren hills.

But it was too late. Men were yelling, at first
disgruntled at being rudely aroused from their
sleep in the cold early hours of the morning.
Helen Rochford stayed rooted to the spot,
praying to hear the voice of a woman among
those of the men. Or, if not, that the men would
return to sleep—each cursing the other for having a nightmare.

Her prayer was not answered for, just as she
had glimpsed the glimmering firelight which
had brought her to a halt, so one of the
awakened men caught sight of the ghostly
whiteness of her frothy nightgown beyond the
fringe glow of the campfire.

This man came for her. A man who snarled at
the other three to be quiet and go back to sleep.
While he went to get himself a woman. They
had snarled at him in turn, and accused him of
being crazy—of having a dream and yelling
aloud in it to wake them.

"I was too terrified to move a muscle, but I
was able to think more clearly than I ever re-

member before," Helen Rochford told her husband and Edge while the half-breed was preparing the chestnut gelding to leave and pick up the trail of the rapists. "And it is all fresh in my mind now. I remember thinking that some evil deity must have intercepted my prayer—about the nightmare, you see?

"But then my nightmare while awake began. The man came to me and asked me what I wanted. The others had seen where he was going and seen me by then. And were quiet. I started to tell him I was running away after I had killed my husband but he would not allow me to finish. He interrupted me to say that he meant what kind of sexual experience I wanted. He did not use the term sexual experience, you understand? He was a good deal cruder than that. The others laughed. He asked me if I wanted to be taken here, or here, or here. Did I want to have one man at a time or more than one. That since I had come to their camp, a woman dressed only in what I was wearing, I was obviously in search of sexual experience.

"While he was saying these things to me— using the Anglo-Saxon expressions, of course— he was forcing me to walk with him toward the camp. With a hand in my hair at the back of my neck. My mind remained absolutely clear, but I felt powerless to resist him. It was as if, too, I had lost the capability to speak.

"One of the men had stirred the fire and added fresh wood. I can remember welcoming the warmth. And remember, too, the filthiness

of the skin on the faces of the men and the
stench of their flesh and their clothing.

"The man continued to hold my hair, here.
While with his other hand he ripped my nightgown where it was tied at the throat. He hurt
me, just as his hand pulling at my hair hurt me.
I knew it would get worse. I knew, too, that my
situation was hopeless. After he had torn my
nightgown off me and thrown it on the fire, I
had decided what I had to do. I would coop-
erate with them. I would be what they wanted
me to be. Do everything that was asked of me.
By so doing, I considered, my suffering would
not be quite so bad. Perhaps they might even
treat me with some degree of kindness. I dared
hope, too, they might take me with them."

The four duster-coated rapists had taken the
trail that went to the southeast of the crag.
Heading for a community called Fallon. The
other fork of the trail led to Tucson. Just
arrowhead marks and the names of the towns
had been chipped in the rockface many years
ago: the distances in miles were not given.

Of much more recent origin was the sign left
by the men who had reached this place along
the Tucson trail, camped for the night, taken
their totally unexpected pleasure with the
woman, abandoned her and then ridden off
down the Fallon trail. And now Edge re-
mounted the gelding and heeled him forward,
over the tracks left by the four horses of the
rapists. Leaving behind him, as the earlier
riders on the trail had left behind them, the

ashes of a fire, the area of grass trampled by hobbled mounts, the elongated impressions in the grass nearby where four men had bedded down, the litter of cans, cigarette butts, wax-paper and a charred fragment of white fabric and the piles of horse and human droppings which marked the spot where Helen Rochford suffered her agony and her anguish.

But the half-breed did not need the visual stimuli of the campsite to trigger vivid recollections of the woman as, in her precise English accented voice, she related the events that took place under the granite rock—her face as expressionless as was the face of the crag while her body remained rigid and she moved quickly only her hands to signal in mime what she could not bring herself to speak.

"I misjudged them. What they required of me was resistance. To intensify their pleasure with me. I could not understand this at the start. When the first one took me the first time. In the normal way. I acted as I thought he would wish. But his pleasure was not complete until he heard me scream in pain when he clawed me—here and here. Then the Negro demanded I turn over. To be taken here. I did so, but he wished for me to kneel so that he could have me as a dog takes a female of the species. I had not understood this and I am sure he intended this to be so. In order that he could wrench at my hair. To force me on to all fours and hold my hair still, in both hands, as he would hold the reins of a horse he was riding.

The third one had me remain on my knees, but upright. So that he could thrust his stinking self into me here. While his hands were like the talons of a bird on my shoulders. And the final man, he was the most brutal of all. The youngest of them, who had been unable to contain himself while he watched the others have me. But he was determined to be proved a man. I was forced to try in so many ways to make him ready to have me, and as each failed, so he hurt me more.

"Eventually, the boy was able to copulate with me. But only in the fullness of time. The last of them to empty his lust into me after the other three had taken me so brutally again. Here and here and here.

"I was totally exhausted by then. Drained of the will to struggle and certainly unable to feign resistance in the way that was demanded. And the boy, denied the pleasure by his own inexperience on the first occasion, felt that I was denying him again. I think perhaps he would have killed me had not the others prevented him. He punched me and he kicked me and I think he was attempting to choke me to death when the others intervened.

"Then that part of it was over and I think I fell into a faint—even a coma—where they left me. I could not see, not even the fire. Could not bring myself to open my eyes, perhaps. But I could hear the men moving. And talking to one another. Hear the horses. There was talk of a man named Fallon they were going to see. In

Tucson. Or perhaps they had come from Tucson. There were some animals they were interested in. With a special brand. Worth a great deal of money. That part is very jumbled in my mind. I think perhaps I kept entering and emerging from the faint, the coma, the exhausted sleep or whatever it was. Certainly I never actually heard them leave. It seemed suddenly as if they had silently vanished. I saw a light. It was the fire. I was naked and shivering with cold, but the embers of the fire went out even as I looked at them.

"I lay there, hoping I would die. Thinking sometimes that I already was dead and I was in hell. But then it began to become light and I was able to see where I was and recognized all of it. Which was when I got up off the ground. It was very difficult. I was in so much pain. And I started back the way I had come. Wanting to die again. Perhaps even hoping that if this country did not kill me—naked as I was—then I would meet up with Mr. Edge and he would do it."

While he rode through the timber and out into the open country of a grassy valley several miles wide, Edge twice went over in his mind the story of the Englishwoman as she had told it to him and to her husband. Did his best to recall it word for word in order for the mental exercise to achieve its purpose. Which was not to decide if Helen Rochford had been raped by four men. Nor even to provide the basis for making an educated guess about whether she had enjoyed even a little some of what had happened to her. Rather, he attempted to either allay or confirm his suspicion—aroused while the woman was telling her tale—that she derived a brand of pleasure from recounting the details of the repeated rapes. To the captive audience of an impotent husband and a man who had refused her advances.

The cause of this suspicion was the way in which she claimed to be confused about her retreat from the wagon and how she made her way back toward it: and yet was able to recall in clear detail every assault upon her body. Or, if she was not able to remember so precisely, she certainly had a vivid imagination and no inhibition about giving it free rein.

But, as he rode down into the northwest to southeast valley, heading for a small town far in the distance, he abandoned his own thoughts of the past. Did so because he realized he could be purposely looking for fuel to fire his dislike of Helen Rochford in a situation where she deserved pity—or in his case, at least indifference. And was searching for it while he ignored the obvious reasonable explanation of why the woman told her story in the way that she did to the two men. Which was to emphasize her determination that the rapists were going to die for the horror, terror, agony, disgust and humiliation they had forced her to endure. And hoped that if she painted a vivid enough word-picture her husband would understand and condone her resolve to kill them herself. And

Edge would have no scruples about selling the men to their killer at a thousand dollars a head.

He tossed away the half-smoked cigarette that had gone out at the side of his mouth and followed it to the trail with a globule of saliva. Not expressing his feelings toward the Englishwoman but instead the self-disgust that he should have to consider so long and so hard how he felt about her. For she should just not have been worth the effort. The four thousand dollars that her husband was going to pay him should be all that mattered to him—until he was close enough to the three white men and the Negro to have to think how to make them his prisoners. Or not so much the money itself. Rather, the length of time such an amount would enable him to live in total freedom. On his own in a country where the noose of convention had not been pulled so tight that a determined man was unable to find a patch of it where his peace—and his peace of mind—was protected by distance from the unwelcome intrusions of his fellowman. Provided he had the wherewithal to purchase such luxury.

But, he decided after reflecting on this prospect for just a few seconds, he was shooting for the moon and did not have a chance in ten million of scoring. With four thousand or four hundred thousand. For if perfection in human life was obtainable in this world, it was surely a condition that had to be ordained by the Creator of the world. And Edge had broken too many of His commandments too many times to

even hope for an occasional nod of acknowl-
edgement from Him.

"Hey, you know, that could be my trouble
lately, horse," he said evenly. "It could be I
haven't been getting my share of adultery."

The gelding, more used to being in the traces
of the wagon than having a rider on his back,
was not overly responsive to the sound of a
voice. Now continued to plod on down the
snaking trail toward the settled area of the
wide valley, head drooping and ears turned
away from the half-breed. But he did vent a
soft snort that could have been of appreciation
when his rider ran a gentle hand down the side
of his neck.

"No sweat, feller. Reason I like most animals
better than most humans is that they can't
help being the way they are. And don't try to
be any different. Or make apology for being
like they are. I thought I was like that. Sure
used to be, but—"

The gelding snorted again. A little louder and
with a raise and toss of his head.

"You want me to be quiet? I'm bothering
you?"

The gelding made no sound outside of the
regular clop of his hooves on the trail as he resumed his servile and disconsolate attitude.

"Yeah, know the feeling," Edge murmured.
"The quiet life's best. Women just don't think
that way though. And there are times when a
man has sore need of a woman."

The coincidence of the animal snorting or

even moving his head as if in response to what the half-breed had said did not occur again. But the sullen wretchedness of his mount served as an opening for the coldly smiling rider to growl:

"Sorry, feller. Real mean of me. Forgot you're a gelding."

Chapter Eight

Several times during the morning ride toward
the small community in the southeast that he
had not seen since he dropped down into the
valley, rain squalls lashed at the increasingly
lush range country spread out around him.
Just once he was hit by a heavy but shortlived
downpour which soaked his clothing and left
him uncomfortably damp for more than an
hour before a wind that had been threatening
under the grey sky since dawn began to curl in
from the north to dry off all that had been sod-
dened by the rain.

The floor of the valley was undulating and at
times rugged. Mostly comprised of vast
expanses of grassland scattered with stands of
mixed timber from grove to forest proportions,
interspersed with areas of red rock hills cut
with ravines and inscribed with fans of scree.
The trail rose and dipped, took wide and sweep-
ing curves, and occasionally turned what came
close to being a right-angle corner: such a trail
across such a piece of country offering a new

and different vista almost every few hundred yards.

But the slow-riding Edge paid no more attention than usual to his ever-changing surroundings. Merely maintained his seemingly casual watch for the first sign that all was not well in the immediate vicinity—while he took note of those details that might well portend trouble at a later time in a different place.

Thus he was aware that he was still in the wake of the four rapists who had left horse droppings, cigarette and cigar butts, an empty match box and several areas of hoofprints on the trail to tell unwittingly of their passing to the interested party behind them. He knew, also, that he was on range that was regularly grazed upon by a great many head of cows. And that the ranch house was a long way off, witnessed by the line shack he passed—too far to the north of the trail to be worth a stop, even though he would have avoided the soaking from the squall had he done so.

But despite the damp and cold, then just cold after the wind had dried him and continued to buffet at him from the side, he nonetheless felt good. Had been long enough out of the disconcerting company of the Rochfords to be free of the self-doubts they had triggered within him. And felt confident of his ability to handle whatever dangerous situation might explode at any turn or beyond any hill crest along the trail— and to adapt to whatever were his circumstances in the wake of fresh violence.

Out of sight, out of mind . . . that was the
only way to be with people who for some inex-
plicable reason acted to cramp a feller's style.
Then, just as he fastened on this thought—and
was about to get angry at himself because, par-
adoxially, it meant he had not ridded his mind
of the Englishwoman—he reached a place
where the four men he was tracking had veered
off the trail. To angle due south toward an ex-
tensive area of rearing red rock and timber—
increasing the pace of their mounts from an
easy walk to a gallop. But whether they had
spurted to catch up with something or to get
somewhere, or suddenly had become the
quarry of somebody other than Edge, the half-
breed was unable to tell. Until, on the fringe of
the expanse of rugged terrain, the sign of the
four horses was seen to be overprinted on other
recently made tracks—left by the cloven
hooves of a bunch of cows set off in a small-
scale stampede.

Now, as he rode in among the rocks and the
timber and the brush, Edge did intensify the
degree of watchfulness he maintained around
him. And, too, actively listened for sounds that
were alien to those made by himself and mount.
But all the time remained conscious of the sign
he was following—so knew at once when he
reached the point where the tracks in front of
him were not left only by a quartet of horsemen
in pursuit of maybe a half-dozen cows. Here,
where the rugged area was again accessible
from the pastureland by means of a gap like a

canyon mouth between two bluffs, several
other horses had joined the chase. Their route,
and the one which Edge now followed on foot
—leading the gelding by the bridle—across a
slope and into a ravine that curved and dropped away sharply. Narrowing to perhaps thirty
feet before it suddenly opened up again on to a
rock-walled ledge that was part of the rim of a
basin that was densely wooded around the rest
of its perhaps three-mile circumference.

From where he waited, watching and listening for a danger signal, a few paces beyond the
point where the ravine began to widen toward
its end, Edge was unable to see the bottom of
the basin. Was just able to glimpse the top of
the column of smoke from a fire down there,
before the wind that blew from behind him and
out across the basin took hold of it and disinte-
grated it.

Elsewhere around the rim of the depression
that he was able to see from where he stood the
ground fell away in a sheer cliff of earth and
rock. With, here and there, a jagged indenta-
tion littered with debris of loose earth and rock
and tree trunks where there had been a landslip. Not so beyond the area of flat rock he now
crossed, after hitching the dejected gelding to
a clump of brush and sliding the Winchester
from the boot—clicking back the hammer with
a thumb the moment he detected the disinte-
grated smoke for what it was.

Long ago—hundreds, thousands or maybe
even millions of years—a massive landslip had

occurred. Or perhaps it had been an earth
tremor that created the basin. Whichever,
there had been a great falling away of loose
ground that was halted only when the immov-
able mass of rock stemmed the collapse. And it
was from the slightly upturned extreme of this
rock that the half-breed was able to watch his
prospect of earning four thousand dollars dis-
appear in much the same way as the smoke at
the top of the column was gusted out of exis-
tence by the wind.

The land that had slid downwards from this
side of the basin so long ago had settled in the
form of an uneven slope, steep in parts but
gentle in others. And in the intervening years
had been seeded by nature with grass and
brush and trees. Thus was the basin a kind of
enormous natural amphitheater with a verdant
audience section looking down upon the deeply
sited stage with a backdrop of towering cliffs.

Which placed the half-breed in the balcony,
able to see both the action at the foot of the
cliffs and the response this was drawing from
the restless witnesses on the slope.

The seven Longhorns that had caught the
attention of the duster-coated quartet had been
finally chased to exhaustion, or into a trap, at
the bottom of the basin. Where they were now
penned by a corral of lariat ropes. Close by the
men's mounts which were hobbled but not unsaddled. While the men themselves—three of
them white and one Negro, just as the Englishwoman had said—were in a half circle around

one side of the fire. Two of them sprawled out on their backs, hats over their faces, while the other two finished scraping food off their plates. Obviously totally unaware that they would soon be in a trap as secure as the one in which the steers were held.

Ten men were in process of springing the trap. At least, that was the number of horses hitched to each other and to the low branch of a tree in a grove some hundred yards to the left and half that distance below where the half-breed stood. The good and strong-looking, well-tended animals left in a place where they were out of sight of the duster-coated men beside the fire. While their riders spread out across the slope and then started down it, cautiously making use of best patches of cover.

At first, Edge could see only six of the men advancing down the slope, for in some cases the brush or trees or small hollows provided total cover from all directions. But eventually he had every man spotted, even if never all at the same time. Each of them at match for the condition of the waiting horses near the grove of trees. Big and strong and in fine shape for hard work. Chaps-wearing cowpunchers with spurs on their heels and sixguns in their holsters. The youngest not yet twenty and the oldest close to sixty, as near as Edge could judge over a distance that widened all the while —the men closing on their objective which was about three quarters of a mile from where he stood. Now crouched, as the Negro finished his

meal, set aside his plate and unfolded out on to
his back—had a view up the broad fan of the
broken slope to the rim of the basin where the
half-breed was positioned, but obviously saw
nothing to arouse his suspicion before he tipped his hat over his face.

The cowpunchers had frozen in their advance
when the Negro shifted his position. Moved
forward and down again as soon as the black
man masked his face with the hat. But after a
minute or so, halted in an arcing line some two
hundred and fifty yards away from and above
the fire. Perhaps nine of them responding to a
signal from the tenth, or maybe pausing at pre-
determined positions. Where, from the attitudes adopted by the seven men Edge was now
able to see, they were prepared to bide their
time for as long as was needed. Each of them
with a clear shot at the four men beside the fire
—and with a good chance of scoring if he used
the repeater rifle he carried, rather than the
revolver which one or two eased nervously
from their holsters and set on the ground
nearby.

Then the fourth duster-coated man was
through with eating and Edge saw signs of
both relief and impatience among the cowpunchers—or perhaps was able only to sense
the reactions of the men in hiding to the moves
of the man at the fire as he finished his meal
and made to stretch out and sleep for awhile.

But then the wind veered suddenly and
gusted more strongly than it had done since

Edge moved in off the open rangeland—to curl over one of the tree topped rims of the basin and drive down into it. To fan the flames of the fire and snatch at three hats which it sent end over end among the abruptly unsettled Longhorns. The trio of men who had been dozing beneath the hats came up off the ground with snarls of anger while the one who had been about to stretch out vented a shrill burst of derisive laughter.

Then the wind backed off from the depths of the basin as abruptly as it had rushed down into there and ten second later abated totally. And only as this happened did Edge discover what a perfect amphitheater was formed by the enormous depression below him—when the foliage of the trees elsewhere around the rim ceased to rustle at what had come close to being a roar and he heard a man snarl:

"The hell with it! Let's get the critters marked and move on out of this spooky place!"

There had been a moment of utter silence before the words were spoken. And a longer period of several stretched seconds passed on without another sound as the men, the animals and even the fire seemed to be transfixed in some kind of limbo where movement and noise were forbidden. Until a log on the fire cracked, a horse whinnied, and steers jostled each other and the Negro growled:

"Spooky's right, Leroy. I ain't never in my life before—"

Edge crouched lower as all four men raked

their fear-filled gazed over the cliff faces and across the slope. This as the black rapist's nervousness expanded to an extent where he was unable to voice any more words that were amplified with perfect clarity to many times their original volume by the nature of the surrounding terrain.

"Son-of-a-bitch!" the youngest member of the quartet said slowly, shuffling around in a full circle. Just a boy, as Helen Rochford had said. Seventeen or eighteen, maybe. A broad grin on his unbristled face as he listened to the odd effect that the arc of cliffs and the facing slope had on his voice.

"I don't friggin' like none of this!" the most senior of the men said, attempting to whisper which served to create an even more eerie sound. "Could be what we're sayin' is reachin' for friggin' miles! Leroy's right, let's get our chores done and hightail it outta here!"

He was the slow eater who had not lost his hat in the gust of wind before the norther ceased to blow. So, the one who had first crack at the Englishwoman after bringing her into the camp in the fork of the trail in the distant timber. Token top hand of the quartet from the way in which the other three went along with his suggestion, then did as he instructed in the matter of preparing for the branding of the Longhorns. Or maybe it was just that he was the brains and they the brawn. And he also had a patently good excuse for not getting involved

in the heavy work—he had a lame right leg that
Helen Rochford had failed to mention.

It appeared to be rigid from above the knee
all the way down to the foot. But this did not
hamper him from sitting close to the fire, one
hand thickly wrapped in rag so that he could
from time to time shift without burning
himself on the two branding irons that Edge
had not noticed were in the fire before. Moving
them from one hot spot in the glowing ashes to
another while the Negro, the boy and a short,
fat, totally bald headed man struggled inex-
pertly to separate one steer from the other six
without allowing all of them to escape the rope
corral.

Which was a snorting and cursing, kicking
and slapping, spitting and sweating episode
the concealed cowpunchers would probably
have relished under different circumstances.
But these experts at handling recalcitrant
Longhorns were in no mood to see the funny
side of what was happening below them: were
more concerned with the possibility of getting
their heads blown off if something should go
wrong with their plan to trap the four duster-
coated men.

Then the three cut one steer out of the bunch
and hustled the frightened animal toward the
fire. The Negro gripping one horn, the boy the
other and the bald headed man hanging on the
tail.

"Not too damn close!" the man with the lame

leg snarled as he got awkwardly to his feet, using one of the branding irons as a supporting crutch. "Don't you crazy fools even know that critters is scared of fire? Get him down right there!"

"Get him down right here the man says, like it was a friggin' itty bitty old rooster we had a hold of to put in the friggin' pot!" the Negro growled sarcastically.

"Quit with the mouth and do it, Toby!" the bald headed Leroy snapped. And tried to knock the animal's hind legs out from under him with a booted foot as he yanked at the tail.

Toby whirled suddenly to give as good as he got, but managed only a glower without venomous words before the steer wrenched his head around in the opposite direction, at the same time as he lashed out with his hind legs to kick at the man tugging on his tail. The Negro left it too late in letting go of the horn and was sent full length to the ground with a yell of alarm that lengthened and changed the key to express pain. This as the kid retained his hold on the other horn and was thudded hard into the shoulder of the steer by the fast and powerful turn of the animal's head. And vented a snarling curse that was matched by one from Leroy who leapt clear of the cloven hooves of the hindlegs but did not release his double-handed grip on the tail.

And, unbalanced, frightened and in pain, the steer crashed heavily down on to his side. Taking the cursing kid with him. Narrowly missing the Negro who dragged himself clear of the tumbling animal just in time.

"That's it!" the lame man yelled in a shrill-voiced excitement as he scampered away from the fire, pulling the glowing iron clear and waving it in the air. "You got him, Sonny! Hold him now! Leroy, get on the critter's ass! Toby, give the kid a hand! Move it now!"

The unfortunate Longhorn was making his own contribution to the bedlam of noise that resounded at such high volume up from the bottom of the acoustically strange basin. And then the animal's cry, changed in tone from terror to agony, became abruptly loud enough to blot out every other sound—even the sizzle of the branding iron as it cooled on the coat, skin and then the tissue as the lame man pressed too hard and too deep against the hindquarter.

When he heard this, saw the smoke and steam rising from the point of the brand and in imagination caught the scent of burnt flesh in his nostrils, the impassive set of Edge's features altered to show a grimace. And he tightened his fisted grips around the frame and barrel of the cocked Winchester as, just for a part of a second, he felt a near-overwhelming compulsion to swing the rifle to the aim and blast a bullet into the man who caused the helpless steer such suffering.

But then the brutal branding was finished. The iron was jerked free, hung with pieces of cooked meat torn from the living animal. The

cry of agony was reduced to a whimper, over
which Leroy snarled as he rose from beside the
distressed Longhorn:

"You are one mean-hearted sonofabitch,
Hayden!"

The kid and the Negro sprang away from the
head of the steer, which struggled to rise just
as fast but was awkward and then unsteady—
obviously disorientated.

"Bein' one of them kinda men is the first step
to gettin' rich!" the lame man answered
through teeth clenched in a vicious grin as he
turned toward the fire. "Which none of us ain't
gonna be unless you guys do your shares of
what needs to be done! So best you put this
critter back behind that rope and bring out
another!"

He stooped to thrust the cooled iron back
into the glowing ashes and then checked that
the other one was ready. This while Leroy
scowled at what the first had done to the hind-
quarters of the steer. And the kid and the
Negro gripped a horn apiece again, to start to
urge the no longer struggling animal back
toward the rope corral.

"Move your ass, Leroy!" the youngest of the
quartet snapped. "Ain't no way to change the
C-bar S brand without goin' deep! Not if it ain't
gonna be spotted by a Selmar hand for a—"

"If you're so friggin' squeamish, Leroy
Engels, you never oughta have gotten in this
business!" the Negro cut in.

While the heated, ill-tempered exchange was taking place, every nuance of the men's voices amplified and emphasized by the sound-box qualities of the basin, Edge shifted his attention to those members of the ambuscade party whom he could see. And saw that they, in turn, were looking towards one of their number who was hidden from his sight—obviously waiting for a signal to make their presence known to the rapists become rustlers.

A signal which came just as the scowling Leroy Engels made an entrance into the rope corral so that Toby and Sonny could lead the subdued Longhorn inside. A silent signal at which every man on the slope rose—all of them in clear view of Edge now. But unseen by the rustlers for a few moments as they remained busy with their chores. Until a man above them called:

"Where there's life there's hope, you thievin' bastards!"

Engels released the rope and the Negro and the kid let go of the steer—all three whirling to look toward the man who had spoken. Each dropping into a half crouch as he clawed aside his duster at the waist. This as the man at the fire turned with less haste, lame leg swinging wide, one hand still gripping the hot iron that was dragged out of the fire.

"Try to draw a gun and get yourselves killed here and now!" the top man among the cowpunchers went on evenly. "Or take your

chances on beatin' the rap in the Fallon court-
house and not gettin' your scrawny necks
stretched!''

"Sonofabitch!" Sonny rasped.

"Bastards!" Toby snarled.

"Aw shit!" Engels growled.

"I'm with you, Mr. Selmar, sir," Hayden said
evenly, allowing the branding iron to fall to the
ground as he raised both arms high in the air.
"While there's life there's—"

"You've gotten to be a little wiser as you got
older, Arch," Selmar interrupted the lame man.
"But not wise enough to know ain't anyone
gets away with rustlin' my stock. You figure
your men wanna die here or take the chance at
Fallon?"

Edge was able to see just the back of the
rancher and from this judged him to be about
the oldest of the ambushers. Was certainly the
shortest and fattest. Aiming a Winchester
from the hip and now raking it away from Arch
Hayden to cover the trio of men at the rope
corral as the Negro snarled:

"We ain't *his* men, mister! We do what we
want and take no account of what he tells—"

"Show the man, Floyd," Selmar said evenly.

"Sure thing, Clark," the cowpuncher at one
end of the arcing line answered. And threw the
stock of his Winchester up to his shoulder,
aligned the sights and squeezed the trigger as
part of a single fluid move.

The report sounded with crystal clarity in
every part of the basin. The same as the cry

that ripped from Toby's lips as the heel of his left boot was partially blasted off. And Floyd vented an amplified grunt of satisfaction as he pumped the action of the repeater to eject the spent shellcase and jack a fresh bullet into the breech. Had no need to provide another exhibition of his marksmanship because the Negro and the two whites flanking him suddenly had their arms high and straight above their heads.

"Fine and dandy," Clark Selmar said in the same even tone he had always used. "Now you understand that you men are *my* men—in a manner of speakin'. Which means you do what I tell you when I tell you."

He turned as if to speak to the men on his right. But then, canting his rifle to his shoulder, he completed a full half turn and tilted back his head. And Edge, knowing he had been spotted, made no attempt to back off the few paces that would have taken him out of the elderly man's angle of vision. Instead, took four steps toward the top of the slope—to show enough of himself so that Selmar could see he was holding the Winchester in an unthreatening attitude across the base of his belly.

"Goes for you up there as well, mister!" the rancher called, raising his voice now. "If you're one of them or have in mind to get your snout in this mess of swill?"

Several of the cowpunchers were as surprised as the rustlers to see the tall, lean man with the rifle up on the rim of the basin. And all these peered hard at the half-breed—with nervous-

ness in some cases and hope in others. Not so
Floyd who remained like a stone statue with
his cocked Winchester at his shoulder. Then
there was a mixture of relief and dejection seen
on the upturned faces as Edge let go of the
barrel and moved the rifle to slope it to a
shoulder—and with his free hand touched the
brim of his hat. Thus acknowledged that
Selmar had first claim to the prisoners before
he backed off from where the men below could
see him, and muttered for his own ears:

"First come gets all there is, I guess. Have to
rustle up something for myself."

Chapter Nine

Back at the mouth of the ravine, the half-breed
swung up into the saddle on the chestnut gelding and slid his Winchester into the boot. Then
chewed on some jerked beef as he listened to
the voices from below—not so distinctly heard
now he was away from the top of the slope—
and watched the smoke of the fire get thicker.
Then he wheeled his mount slowly and started
back the way he had come: as easy riding and
cautiously alert as before. Just briefly and
without resentment envious of Clark Selmar
and his men who were going to boil up some
coffee before they set off with their prisoners
and the evidence of rustling for Fallon.

Just off the trail to the distant town, Edge
found a stand of timber in which he was able to
watch from cover for the captors and captives
to emerge from the expanse of rock-rugged
country which fringed the basin: this over a
distance of some mile and a half. And, perhaps
an hour and a half after he lowered his rump on
to a tree root and leaned his back against the

trunk, he saw the men ride out from between flanking cliffs.

Selmar was at the front of the column which moved at an easy trot, with the duster-coated quartet of prisoners two abreast behind him. Then came the nine C-bar-S hands: eight of them riding in a double file while the odd man brought up the rear—the steer with the changed brand on a lead line behind him.

There was an almost cavalry-like orderliness about the formation and its progress toward and then along the trail. An impression that was heightened by the uniform style of the riders' garb—ten of the men attired in the outfits of working cowpunchers that varied so little one from another while the other four looked even more like troopers in their identical dusters. Albeit dejected by defeat as they rode in the custody of the victors, shoulders slumped and heads hung low. Astride mounts that were roped together, both side by side and front to rear. The woebegone attitudes of Hayden, Engels, the Negro and the kid emphasized by the obvious sense of triumph that was being experienced by the rancher and his hands.

Edge was about to lead the gelding deeper into the timber as the column drew close, but a dark cloud that had been threatening rain for almost an hour suddenly let loose a downpour to restrict visibility and deaden sound. And the deluge acted, too, to wash out all recent signs on the trail—signs that Edge knew the watchful Clark Selmar had spotted. Left most recently by the chestnut gelding, the hoof-prints of the horse superimposed on the tracks made—also not too long ago—by a four-wheeled wagon with a pair of animals in the traces.

The rain ceased as abruptly as it had started, but the wind that came with it continued to blow as the half-breed moved off in the wake of the column. And for the rest of the afternoon and into early evening the norther did not let up. While, at irregular intervals, low scudding clouds—near black against the unmoving grey-ness above them—unleashed short and sharp, flesh stinging showers of icy rain.

During much of this time, Edge could not al-ways see the men he was following. But he did see them frequently enough—and from close enough—to know that the cowpunchers were all still in the column. That one or more had not been ordered by Selmar to break away and check if the unknown man at the rim of the basin was still close by. While, when the stead-ily riding bunch was out of sight, the rain-softened ground only ever temporarily failed to show sign: for the most part retained clear im-pressions of hoofprints.

It was a cold and uncomfortable ride across the broad and shallow valley, but the half-breed had no reservations about what he was doing there as he sat his saddle with the collar of the sodden sheepskin coat turned up to brush the brim of a hat that often spilled rainwater with the slightest movement of his

head. The chance of him earning four thousand
dollars was all but blasted away when the shot
from Floyd's rifle caused all four rapists to
surrender to Clark Selmar. And with every
yard that was covered toward due process of
law at Fallon the odds against the prisoners
making a successful escape grew longer. But
that ever more slender chance did exist, and he
intended to be close enough to take advantage
of such a turnabout if it should happen.

And if it did not, then Fallon would probably
serve as an adequate substitute for Tucson in
terms of supplying him with what he needed to
ride the next trail. And also, the Rochfords
would surely be waiting in town: to see that he
had not fallen down on the job they gave him.
Had simply been beaten to the punch, but
stayed with it until the last chance to win was
gone.

He suddenly spat viciously down at the trail,
just as another squall lashed out of the
ominous dusk sky. And against the roar of the
wind in his ears and the hiss of rain on the
ground he snarled:

"You crazy Mex bastard! You got no business giving a shit about what she thinks of
you!"

He spat again and then shook his head as if
he needed to make an effort to force the scowl
off his face and replace it with the usual impassive set. After this, it seemed that he rode
for a very long time through a shallow sea of
mud that was constantly pocked by teeming

raindrops. But then, as he emerged from this period of intense concentration upon the demanding process of shutting his mind to thoughts of the blue-eyed, blonde-haired, slim-bodied Englishwoman he knew he had not been detached from his surroundings for as long as it had appeared while he struggled to reestablish his self-control. For he could still see the rain-marked trail as the squall moved away, so there was the murky light of dusk left in the Arizona evening. For a few more seconds, anyway: until full night was clamped down between the unbroken sky and the sodden land.

The norther tugged a final time at man and mount, then suddenly dropped. And in the surrounding silence the splashing hoofbeats of the gelding over the liquid ground sounded as eerily loud as had the voices of the men in the basin. While it was not possible to tell if the pitch darkness of the moonless and unstarred night merely created an impression that the unmoving air was colder than the norther had been or whether the temperature actually had dropped several degrees. Certainly, the half-breed in the cold, rain-drenched clothing knew that it was only in his imagination that the smell of smoke through the dampness and the glimmering of a number of lights against the darkness in the distance stirred a sensation of warmth somewhere deep inside him. As he relished in anticipation whatever mild degree of comfort was available in the promised shelter of the town of Fallon.

Closer to the actuality of warmth and dry-
ness, Edge reined the gelding to a halt and
peered down the slope over the final mile between himself and the community as he took
out the makings and rolled and lit a cigarette.
And in the time this required, decided he was
totally in control of his own reflexes. Both physical—he was able to peer into the night in
every direction and know he was seeking a
threat and had the capability to deal better
than most men of his age with any kind of
sudden attack. And mental—he had admitted
to himself that he lusted for the body of the
sensual Englishwoman, did not regret scorning
her in the circumstances that existed then but
would not refuse her advances if the opportunity came again.

"A bastard attracted to a bitch and vice
versa, I figure," he murmured to the horse as
he heeled the gelding forward toward the glimmering lights.

The animal offered no response—did not
even raise his ears.

"The world is full enough of our kind," he
added, peering across the darkness shrouded
range to the left and the right and over his
shoulder. "Hello, a no-strings screw and goodbye. It should be easy, shouldn't it?"

The chestnut gelding splashed steadily on
down the sloping trail, surefooted and reliable.
Not needing to be steered, maybe because in
his equine imagination he was savoring the
warmth and the food and the rest that he

sensed was waiting for him among the lights of Fallon. And Edge grinned with his teeth clenched to the cigarette as he continued to watch for trouble in the darkness and said:

"You're supposed to tell me it would only be easy if I was as much of a bastard as I think I am, feller." Then he sighed and ran a hand gently down the side of his mount's neck as he added: "You ain't much of a conversationalist, are you? But that's okay since I ain't usually much of a talker myself."

He was almost up to the point where the open trail became the building-flanked street of a town that was larger than it had looked— both from back on the distant valley side and from the impression he received when he began to head for the cluster of glimmering, then gleaming lights. From far off the notion of the place being small had been based upon the false premise that since he had never heard of the town of Fallon it could not be of any significant size. While from closer range he had been led astray by the assumption that the entire community was huddled within the confines of the lamplight—whereas, when he rode in off the trail he was at the northwestern end of a street that was in darkness for more than a half mile.

A dangerous darkness, he suddenly realized —but revealed no visible sign of his discovery as he continued to ride, apparently easy in the saddle, between the high facades of two barns. And it required an expert to spot that there was anything to be mistrusted in the way he let

go of the reins with his right hand and seemingly absently scratched his thigh—so that he
was only a half second away from sliding the
Winchester out of the forward hung boot.

"Freeze, son!" an expert snapped and Edge
instantly recognized him from his voice as
Clark Selmar.

The half-breed used his left hand to rein in
the gelding, as he pushed the part-smoked cigarette with his tongue from between his teeth
so that it angled from the side of his lips. This
as he closed his lids to the narrowest of slits
and peered at the mouth of an alley between
the barn and an equally dark, less high building
beside it.

"Fine and dandy," the rancher said, less stri-
dently. "Want you now to put your hands up
behind your neck and join the fingers, son.
Way you would if you was sittin' in your very
favorite armchair after a hard day's chores."

Edge released the reins from his left hand
and brought this up with his right to do as he
was instructed. Only then felt the tension generated by others drain out of the incident, as he
continued to peer at the alley from which the
short and overweight Selmar stepped, his
hands thrust deep into the pockets of a dark-
colored oilskin coat.

"Something, feller.'

"You say it, son."

"Sitting like this because I've already seen
your top gun do his stuff."

"Floyd's the C-bar-S foreman, son. Hired on

as such and just happens to know how to handle a rifle."

"Has me covered now, I figure?"

"You bet your ass he has," Selmar confirmed evenly as he halted twenty feet in front of and slightly to the right of where Edge sat unmoving astride the statue-like gelding.

"He shows himself, it better not be with his rifle still aimed at me. Unless he's ready to kill me. On account of I'll sure as hell be fixing to kill him."

"Talks big, as well as to himself, Clark!" a man called in a derisive tone from the roof of the building on the other side of the alley from the barn.

"Don't they say that a guy talkin' to himself is showin' the first sign of goin' nuts?" another man asked, rhetorically sardonic. He was positioned in the cracked open doorway of the barn to the left, directly to the side of where the half-breed sat his mount on the center of the street.

"You run off at the mouth too much, Whitney!" Selmar snapped, with a cursory glance over his shoulder toward the flat roof of the single-story building. Then he peered for longer at the front of the barn across the street to warn: "And you're already crazy, Floyd, if you don't take this man seriously."

"Aw, Clark, come on—" Floyd started to complain sourly.

At the same time as Whitney growled: "Hell, I'm just lettin' the stranger know he ain't got just the one Selmar hand—"

"Shut up the both of you!" the man in the open cut in.

"One thing about talking with a horse like this one, feller," the half-breed said into the silence that was permeated with disgruntlement. "Never does answer back."

"Like a couple of answers from you, son?"

Edge had finished his narrow-eyed scanning of the darkened area of town where he was forced to halt: decided there were only the two men close by to back up the rancher. And now he peered toward the illuminated section of Fallon as he supplied:

"The four fellers you caught branding your steers raped a woman, Selmar. Back in the timber beyond the valley where this trail and the one to Tucson meet. She wanted me to see they got what's coming to them for what they did to her. Knowing they've been hanged will maybe be good enough for her. Won't matter what they're hanged for officially. They can only die the once. That about cover it?"

There was some activity at the well-lit center of town, but this street and the corners of the ones that intersected it were not thronging with citizenry. Perhaps because the night air was too damply chill for strolling and the places of entertainment and commerce extended a warm welcome that was too tempting to refuse. Or maybe it was that the portents of dangerous trouble kept all but the most foolhardy curious off the streets.

"How do I know that ain't all hogwash, son?" Clark Selmar asked, his tone lacking conviction. "Way you been followin' me and my boys with the prisoners, seems to be you could be lookin' for a way to spring the rustlers loose?"

Edge spat the dead cigarette butt off his lower lip and answered: "Was making sure they didn't get loose themselves, feller. And if they did, they didn't stay that way."

"Well, son, you can quit worryin' on that score now. Because that double-dealin' Arch Hayden and his cronies are locked up real tight in Jack O'Rouke's jailhouse."

"That's fine, feller," the half-breed drawled. "Just the one thing I have to worry about now."

"There is?"

"You told me to freeze while ago. If I stay out here like this much longer, it's what I could do."

"Okay, on your way," Clark Selmar allowed. "But if it is hogwash you been givin' me and you try grabbin' them thievin' bastards out of Jack O'Rouke's place, you'll wind up real cold, son. Real quick. Buried in the ground as deep as you're tall."

Edge lowered both his hands and took up the reins from where they rested across the saddle-horn. Heeled the gelding forward.

"That's tellin' him, Clark!" Whitney yelled in admiration from the building roof as the half-

breed rode by. "Buried deep as he's tall.
Reckon there ain't nothin' so freezin' cold as a
grave in the ground."

"Hey, cool it, Whitney!" Floyd called as he
stepped out of the barn, the door swinging
open a little wider with an eerie creaking sound.
He held his repeater in a one-handed grip at his
side, barrel canted down toward the rain-
softened street surface. A tall, thin, slicker-
coated man with a gaunt and darkly stained
face whose tone of voice revealed he shared in
his boss's opinion of the half-breed now—even
before he went on: "Like Clark says, I reckon
we oughta take this guy real serious. Close to,
he looks like a real mean character."

Whitney rose to reveal himself in dark silhouette against the only slightly less dark
backdrop of the sky above the roofline of the
building. Shorter and stockier than Floyd. Not
wearing any kind of topcoat or hat now the rain
was finished. Both his hands held low down in
front of him, gripping the butt of a revolver
that was aimed between his feet and glinted
dully in the faint level of light that reached him
from the mid-town area. His hair showed as
blond or even white in the same fringe glow.

"Don't be a fool!" Selmar snapped over his
shoulder. "Do like Floyd told you!"

The attitude of the man on the roof had been
tautly aggressive when he first showed himself. Now he shrugged.

"The boss and the foreman, stranger," he
called down in a rasping tone as Edge rode by

him, the impassive-faced man astride the gelding shifting his head to look from the C-bar-S hand at the front of the barn to the one on the roof of the building across the street. "So I gotta do like they say. I'm cool, but I ain't shiverin'—you know what I mean?"

Edge nodded and answered in an even-toned voice: "A fair shake is what we all want."

Chapter Ten

The building on top of which Whitney had been standing had a sign painted on each window that flanked the porched doorway announcing it housed the headquarters of the Fallon Cattlemen's Association: and before Edge had advanced very far along the town's main street, Clark Selmar and his two hands had entered the place and lit a lamp that spilled a shaft of bright light from one of the windows.

By this time, the irritating itch between the half-breed's shoulder blades had dulled and he was aware of being watched once more—but there was no sensation of threat in the new survey, which was being made from a corner on the first intersection of this side of town. Some hundred yards from where he had been ordered to halt by Selmar, so within earshot of what had been said. That distance closer to the well-lit area of Fallon—where more people were moving in view now—but still only on the fringe of the light.

Edge rode by a bank, the office of a newspaper called the *Fallon Advocate*, a small chapel and a large house. Like the two barns, the place the trio of men had entered and the feed and grain store across from this, all the buildings were of frame construction and had been put up several years earlier. Beyond the intersection, and along the streets that went off to either side, the buildings were of more recent origin and used a wider range of materials. A mixture of residential and commercial premises, spaced wider apart than the group that seemed to have been all the town had consisted of for a long time.

"Guess the newspaper office was something else in the old days," the half-breed said as he started across the intersection, and glanced only briefly at the side of the small chapel with its truncated belfry. And added, as the man stepped away from the wall so that he was seen a little more clearly in the fringe of the light: "Sheriff?"

"The *Advocate's* always been here, Mr . . .?"

"Edge," the half-breed supplied and looked more closely at the lawman who angled out across the intersection to draw level with the gelding and fall in beside it. Saw a man of fifty or so with a weather-stained and life-lined face that was as long and lean as his own. But was dark eyed as well as dark skinned, with a weaker jaw and a much thicker moustache that did not droop to either side of his small mouth. About five feet ten inches tall with a muscular build beginning to thicken with middle-age fat. The man dressed in a city-style but country made suit of dark-hued, rough-textured fabric that looked to be in need of pressing—perhaps only since the rain of the day had drenched it. He also wore a vest, a dark-colored shirt and a tie—the vest and the tie grey like his wide-brimmed Stetson. So that the brightest thing about his appearance was the five-pointed metal star in a circle that was pinned to the breast pocket of his crumpled suit jacket—on the upper slope caused by the bulge of the gun he carried in a shoulder holster.

"Mr. Edge. Since when Fallon was just the Selmar ranch and a handful of little homesteads. Those days, the paper didn't sell more than a couple of dozen copies, but Otis Selmar —that was Clark's father—he used to make up the losses. In the same way he had the chapel built and paid for a preacher to be here. Believed that people who lived out on the frontier shouldn't be shut off from the rest of the world. And should have easy access to religious guidance if they felt the need. Education, too. The building that is now the Fallon Bank was a school able to take up to twenty pupils when it was first erected. I'm extremely pleased there was no serious trouble with Clark Selmar, Mr. Edge."

Sheriff Jack O'Rouke spoke like a man who had been educated at a fine school a great many miles to the east and north of the one he and Edge passed now, across from the court house—both buildings of white stone set back from the street behind neatly trimmed lawns bisected by cement walks. Was from one of the New England states, the half-breed guessed, the burr almost gone from his voice but the breeding still clearly discernible.

"No sweat."

"And I trust there will be no more trouble concerning the prisoners I am holding in the jailhouse, Mr. Edge?"

"I caused some already?"

"Indirectly. The multiple rape of which you spoke to Clark took place outside the valley, as I understand you."

"Right."

"Which places the crime outside my area of jurisdiction. If the lady concerned wishes to press charges, representations should be made to the law office in Tucson. We strive to see that justice is done by due process of law in this area, Mr. Edge."

The mounted half-breed and the lawman walking alongside the gelding had reached the center of Fallon's nighttime activity now, and Edge saw he had been wrong to think of it as the mid-town section. For, in fact, it was at the southeastern end of the main street which, beyond the oasis of light and movement in the darkness, curved away due south through the night across the rolling hill country of the valley bottom similar to that he had ridden over during the rainy afternoon.

"Does Selmar money pay for that due process as well as the church and the school—"

O'Rouke's urbanity abruptly vanished as he

shot out a hand to catch hold of the gelding's bridle. And he glared with scowling eyes up into the heavily bristled face of the half-breed, teeth bared as he rasped:

"I was elected by the citizens of Fallon and I'm paid out of civic funds, mister! And you better believe me! I was down the street doing my sworn duty! Which means that if there had been criminal gunplay, I would have done my level best to see the guilty party or parties were brought to justice."

Edge consciously needed to make the effort to suppress his anger at this man who for a few seconds had control of his horse. And knew, from the way in which O'Rouke snatched his hand away from the bridle, that the Fallon lawman had glimpsed the depth of feeling which had been directed down at him from the slivers of glinting blue that were the half-breed's eyes —and the lawman had, in turn, to concentrate hard on not showing his fear.

"My mistake if one was made, feller. When I see the lady, I'll tell her about Tu—"

"A mistake was made, Mr. Edge," the lawman cut in and now it was obvious he had to work hard at checking anger—at himself and Edge—in the wake of diminished fear. "But I can understand how it happened. I should, perhaps, have made my presence known at the same time Clark Selmar did. But being on the side of the right does not always make a man do the right thing. Good evening to you, and I hope you enjoy your stay in our town."

"Obliged, sheriff," Edge answered, and responded to O'Rouke's tip of the hat with a similar gesture of his own, before the crumple-suited man turned and moved back along the darkened length of the street—heading for the brick built jailhouse which had no painted sign to announce what it was, but had barred windows and the upper part of a gallows showing above the fence around the yard out back to make its function obvious.

Edge paid only scant attention to the departing figure of O'Rouke—and to the trio of men coming along the street from the now darkened Catttlemen's Association building. And he had already seen, as he drew closer, that Fallon's brightly lit but far from noisy nightlife was centered upon the Palace Saloon and the Gourmet Restaurant that was directly opposite each other. Both these were doing good business from the way in which their windows were fogged by condensation. Both having drawn some of their patrons from the earlier customers of the stores which were now starting to close for the night. Hardware and grocery, a bakery and a meat market, a hat shop and a toy shop. Already closed was a gunsmith, the barbering parlor and the bath house.

Riding between the facades of the business premises, Edge was conscious that he was still of interest to the people of the street—men, women and a few children—who were loading supplies on to wagons, moving from one store to another with laden baskets, conversing in

small groups, or already starting for home in
all directions: on foot, astride horses and
aboard rigs. Ordinary-looking, small-town
people who were neither wealthy nor poverty
stricken, in every age group from youth to old
age. Living a good life in this lush Arizona
valley to which trouble was no doubt an infre-
quent visitor. Apprehensive then, when they
saw how some of their number reacted to the
appearance of this stranger so soon after the
quartet of cattle rustlers had been brought to
town and locked in the jailhouse. Their minds
set almost to rest when the threat of blazing
guns between the stranger and the C-bar-S men
faded. And confident that the continued peace
and safety of Fallon and its people was fully
restored after their lawman had said what he
had to—in no uncertain terms, from the way he
took a hold of the stranger's horse and made
him listen. So that now there was merely mild
curiosity in the surreptitious glances sent in
the half-breed's direction as he angled across
the town's main intersection to head for the
two-story Fallon House Hotel sited some two
hundred yards along the quiet side street: the
people who were interested at all in him were
simply intrigued by why this travel-stained
man in the rain-sodden clothing should have
caused such a stir by his entry into town.

Edge could understand why this should be,
but then he paid no further attention to those
who wondered about him—as he put his back
to the peering eyes and rode at the same easy

pace as before toward the brick and timber
hotel which had a jutting sign above the
second floor balcony advertising its name and
the fact that it offered ROOMS, BATH,
LIVERY SERVICE. Under the sign, which
like the rest of the building was in dire need of
repainting, the Rochford's covered wagon was
parked. The mules were out of the traces and
the rear off-side corner was jacked up on
blocks, the wheel removed.

Light from an upper floor window illuminated the sign and also spilled across the balcony and down on to the familiar wagon. This
was augmented at street level by a little more
light that escaped from the draped windows
and opaque glass panels of the double doors to
the lobby. Doors which were jerked open
abruptly to lay a much brighter wedge of light
across the stoop and over the wagon as Edge
dismounted from the gelding. At the center of
which was the elongated shadow of a man who
stepped across the threshold and then came to
an abrupt halt with a gasp. A tall and thin, old
and sallow-skinned man who looked like he was
irritable for most of the time—not just when he
was in a hurry.

"You startled me, sir!" he snapped when he
had composed himself. "Which is not good for
anybody, let me tell you! Especially not good
for somebody of advanced years! Who on this
occasion is already agitated at having cause to
leave a fine supper unnecessarily!"

He was hatless, wore a smoking jacket,

baggy pants and carpet slippers. No tie and one side of his starched collar had escaped the stud and was sticking up under his ear. In one hand he was clutching the black, bulky bag of a medical man while the other was pressed to the left side of his chest.

"If you want a second opinion, doc, I figure you'll live," Edge told the vexed old man evenly as he hitched the reins of the gelding to the railing of the stoop.

"I was not joking!"

"Guess that ain't your way. Same as scaring people to death ain't mine."

The doctor dropped his free hand to his side and did a double take at the half-breed. Then grunted and scowled as he moved away from the threshold, across the stoop and down the steps. And looked hard at Edge again as he swung around him, close to—snapped:

"Yes, your kind prefer the more reliable methods, if I am not deceived! So I will be prepared for a call on my services for the duration of your stay in Fallon, young man!"

Then he hurried off along the street, heading for the intersection, his soured attitude to the world in general—and no longer Edge in particular—emphasized in every movement of his frame and limbs.

"Evenin' to you, mister," a woman greeted cheerfully from the open doorway of the hotel. "Don't pay no attention to Doc McCall. His trouble is that he's as mad as they come, but since he's the only one around here got the qualifications to say if a person's crazy, ain't nothin' can be done about him. You want a room?''

Edge looked from the angrily striding form of McCall to the full-blown, provocatively posed figure of the painted-faced, blond-haired, perfume-smelling woman of forty some who stood in the doorway—displaying a smile that had perhaps been alluring twenty or even fifteen years ago.

"A room, a bath and a livery for my horse, ma'am," the half-breed answered. "Just what the sign says."

"And like the sign says, mister," she said, moving her body so that the red dress she wore more closely contoured her large breasts and broad hips, "a room, a bath and a livery is all you get at Rosie Shay's place since a long time gone. I've risen above the old ways of the old days. But some habits die hard."

She straightened up from the doorframe and the whore's smile altered into something close to an embarrassed grin. As Edge drew back his lips to reveal his teeth in a grin of his own that used to be ice cold—lately got something close to warmth into the slitted eyed—and answered:

"Ain't much that is like it used to be, Rosie. Heard tell how these days doctors don't make house calls."

Chapter Eleven

The Rochfords had a second story room at the rear of the Fallon House Hotel, Rosie Shay told Edge without him needing to ask. All he did say to her was:

"Like to get my horse in the stable before I get fixed up myself, Rosie."

"My livery's across the street and a couple of buildin's along, mister. But I'll take care of your animal if you want to get yourself settled in and cleaned up some. You can take any room in the place that's got a number on the door. Exceptin' for seven upstairs at the back. Couple that come to town aboard this wagon got that one. Poor man had some kinda accident that hurt his eyes—made him blind. Doc McCall that was just up to see him says as how maybe the unfortunate man will be able to see again. If he gets the right kinda treatment. Which can't be had no place around here. Maybe closest place is some hospital back east.

" 'Best we can do here is let him rest quiet until he's strong enough to do some more travellin', is what Doc McCall says. Englishman, he is. And got a wife the same. Talk real well, the both of them. Like they was out of the very top drawer, you know what I mean? But if you ask me, she ain't no better than she should be. When they reaches here, it's just before a buckled up wheel on the wagon was about to give out and collapse. Her and me get her husband who's out like a light up to my quietest room and then she seems to be more concerned about the busted wheel than the man.

"I have to tell her where she can find Silas Reeves who's Fallon's blacksmith and wheelwright. And ladykiller, you know what I mean? Silas Reeves don't only come with her to take off the wheel. He takes her off as well. Leavin' me to fret about her poor husband. Who lays quiet for awhile, but then comes outta it and starts to moan with the pain. Which frightens me, mister. On account of I think that maybe he'll die. And dead people give me the creeps. So I goes runnin' for Doc McCall, but by the time he gets back here with me, Mr. Rochford is passed out again. And Doc McCall can't do nothin' except say the Englishman has gotta see some special eye doctor. Then he bawls me out for disturbin' his lousy supper . . . and I'm takin' too damn much which is what a person on her own is inclined to do when there's a willin' listener. But a person that's on her own don't ever have anythin' of interest to say. Aw, shit, I'll go put your horse in the livery."

The half-breed had unsaddled the gelding while Rosie Shay directed the fast-spoken bar-

rage of words at him, the expression on her
fleshy and over-painted face rapidly changing
to match her subject. Then, with the saddle
under one arm and the bedroll draped over the
other shoulder, he waited patiently at the foot
of the steep steps for her to finish. Which she
did, with another embarrassed grin.

"Obliged," Edge said as she came down the
steps and he went up them.

"Bath house is out back, mister. Guess the
fire'll be nearly out now. Lit it in the event the
English couple . . . aw shit, there I go again!"

She took hold of the reins, unhitched them
from around the railing and led the horse
around the rear of the jacked-up wagon and
across the street. While Edge crossed the stoop,
entered the hotel and experienced the pleasant
touch of stove-heated air against the heavily
bristled flesh of his face. This wafted into the
small lobby through an open doorway to one
side. From a stove in a corner of what was obviously the one-time whore's living quarters—
where she had been sitting in a comfortable
armchair close to an ornate lamp, knitting a
shawl, before the pained moans of a badly
injured man interrupted her.

Geoffrey Rochford was quiet now, and the
only sounds in the hotel were made by the
flames in the stove and the footfalls of Edge—
as he veered away from the inviting-looking
scene beyond the open doorway to Rosie
Shay's room and headed for the closed door in

the rear wall of the lobby. Beyond this there was a windowless room that, with the door closed at his back, felt luxuriously warm. For the fire in its stove had not yet gone out—gave off a faint glow from the grate and caused wisps of steam to rise from the undisturbed surface of the large pot of water on its top. There was a kerosene lamp suspended from the ceiling, but Edge did not light it. Instead, stirred the ashes into more forceful life and in their brighter glow transferred the water from the pot to a hip bath. Stripped himself naked except for the beaded thong and razor pouch at his neck and sat for maybe a full two minutes in the off-the-boil but nonetheless still steaming water—with his eyes closed, his lips drawn back in a grin and his nude body totally unmoving. Wallowing in the sheer pleasure of feeling warm, unthreatened and at ease. Then he soaped himself all over, and rinsed off all the suds except for those on his face—which he scraped off along with the bristles. Needed no mirror as he drew the blade of the straight razor over his flesh with the deft and fast movements of long practice.

Then he tipped the scummed water from the tub into a drain in the corner beside the stove and just for a moment or so regretted he had no fresh clothes to put on after drying himself and finger-combing his hair. But although his crumpled and trail-dirtied clothing struck damply chill against his flesh, at least when he stepped out of the bath house he felt considerably better than when he went in thirty minutes earlier.

Rosie Shay had obviously been waiting and listening for him to emerge, for she opened the door of her private room as soon as he stepped into the lobby.

"Horse has got feed and water and a dry stall, mister," she reported. "As a widow woman on her own, I usually eat the the Gourmet Restaurant unless I'm havin' somethin' cold. As cheap and less trouble than cookin' for one. But if you want a home-cooked meal, I'll be happy to—"

"Just what the sign says, Rosie," Edge cut in on her as he started up the stairs that angled up the side wall across from where the lonely woman stood on the threshold of her company-lacking room, trying to conceal the melancholy dejection she felt behind a too-bright smile.

"The customer's always right, mister. And it's the truth. Home cookin' kinda has to be cooked in a home, don't it? And this place ain't neither a house nor a home. Now when Harry Shay brought me here from that crib at San Antone and . . . aw shit, there I go again."

Edge had reached the top of the stairs and was out of sight. And thus did not see the tears that spilled down the artificially pink cheeks of the woman as she closed the door and faced up again to the desolation that was made worse because of the times that had been so much better. He merely heard the sob that she was unable to keep from blurting out of her throat until after the door was closed—and this meant no more to him than had her words.

Just a low level of light from the ceiling hung lamp in the center of the lobby reached up the stairway and part way along the landing that ran from one side of the building to the other at its center—with four rooms at either side. Number seven was the second room down on the right, directly across the landing from number three: into which Edge stepped briefly to set down his saddle and bedroll before he entered the Rochfords' room without knocking.

Both rooms were furnished precisely the same with a double bed, a closet, a bureau, two straight back chairs, a rug at the foot of the bed and a framed picture on the wall above the head of the bed. The walls were painted white, like the ceiling. Thus were the rooms as spartanly comfortable and as reasonably clean as transient guests could expect of a hotel in a town like Fallon.

Geoffrey Rochford was totally oblivious to the conditions of his surroundings as he lay in the very center of the bed, on his back with his head on a pillow and just the narrow shoulders of his tall and skinny frame not covered by the linen and blankets of the bedclothes. The local doctor, despite being in a bad mood, had dressed the wound on the Englishman's forehead and had done so expertly, the bandage that encircled the head as starkly white as the pillowcase: both contrasting vividly with the

darkly bristled face of the unconscious man
who breathed shallowly but regularly.

It was cold in the room and Edge rearranged
the bedclothes enough so that they covered the
naked shoulders of Rochford. He felt strangely
self-conscious as he did so, and continued to be
ill at ease until he was out on the landing again
with the door to room seven closed. Where he
remained for as long as it took to roll and light
a cigarette, when he went back down the stairway, making no attempt to move quietly in the
hotel that was so hushed he could hear the click
of the needles as Rosie Shay continued to knit
the shawl.

Out on the street, where the night air struck
seemingly much colder than before, there was
more noise: that rose in volume as he got closer
to the intersection of this street with the main
one. Not raucous noise—just a kind of hum
that people in a crowd generate with talk and
movement. In this case trickling out under and
over the batwing doors of the Palace Saloon at
a constant low key pitch against the mournful
counterpoint of a guitar being strummed by a
player who seemed not quite sure of the
melody.

The saloon and the restaurant across from it
were now the only places open for business in
Fallon's downtown area—and the light that escaped from them made the neighboring
premises appear that much more dark and
empty by contrast. While the lights that
gleamed at some windows of distant buildings

—houses and, Edge thought, maybe the jail—showed up much more brightly along the traffic-free streets on which he walked alone. Then appeared even more bright in the clean air of night after rain when, as he came within a few feet of the door of the restaurant, its misted up windows were abruptly darkened—a few seconds later while he stood still and vented a low sigh on a stream of cigarette smoke, first one and then another bolt were shot at the foot and the top of the door.

"It's nothing personal, Edge," a man assured evenly as the half-breed turned around to face the doorway of the saloon from which the comment was spoken. "They always close up the restaurant this time every night. If she takes to you, Rosie Shay ain't averse to fixin' a man up with a meal."

"She's just made the offer, Mr. Selmar," the half-breed told the short, overweight rancher who seemed to be a little unsteady on his feet as he pushed out through the batwings—and would have been hit in the back by the swinging doors had not Floyd and Whitney been behind him to each catch hold of one.

"But you didn't have the fancy for what Rosie might force on you for dessert, uh?" Selmar growled, and vented a gust of belly laughter that confirmed he was drunk.

"Celebrating bringing in the rustlers?" Edge countered as he started for the saloon entrance.

"You bet," the tall and thin, guant-faced Floyd answered.

"But you ain't missed nothin', stranger," the shorter and stockier, white-haired Whitney added in a harsh tone that matched his scowl. "You didn't have no invite to the party."

Clark Selmar and his foreman had been happily drunk. And now they became suddenly sourly sober: as both swung to glare at the aggressively challenging Whitney. Floyd was first to snap:

"Damn you, you crazy—"

"Shut up, Floyd!" his boss snarled, and even thrust out an arm as if he expected one of his men to direct more than just words at the other. Then: "What is it with you, Whitney? You tired of livin'? You're a cowpuncher is all. This guy's a gunslinger if ever I seen one. And all you want to do is goad him into a shoot-out. Whatever business we had with him is concluded. To my satisfaction and I guess to his."

Edge closed unhurriedly on the doorway of the saloon with the three men standing close together out front of it.

"Ain't that right, Edge?" Selmar demanded in the same tone of voice, head coming around so that he was looking at the half-breed.

"Some of it, feller. I ain't a gunslinger. Be obliged now if you and your hands will step aside so I can get me a drink."

"Sure thing. Fine and dandy. And don't pay no mind to what Whitney says. You have your first drink on me. Gesture of appreciation for your cooperation in the matter of them four rustlers."

"You got them fair and square so I didn't do you a favor, feller. So nothing's owed. Night to you."

Selmar backed away from in front of the bat-wings and his still outstretched arm forced Floyd to do the same—the older man looking a little irritated that his offer had been declined while the one twenty years his junior and a head taller expressed a worried frown—and attempted to direct a tacit message to the man he was concerned for. But Whitney was not about to be dissuaded from the course of action he had elected to follow from the moment the other two C-bar-S men backed off.

"Night to you, and sweet dreams," he rasped—and made as if to turn away so that Edge would have direct access to the saloon entrance. But instead, he started to swing in the opposite direction just a part of a second later—bringing up his right hand clenched into a prominently knuckled fist.

Clark Selmar groaned: "Oh, God."

"What do you want me—" Floyd started to ask shrilly.

Edge had not expected the smaller man to throw a punch and was momentarily caught off guard. Before he brought up both hands to his face—as if to protect it against the powering right uppercut. But instead, the move was offensive rather than defensive—and he swayed backwards from the waist to draw his jaw out of the path of the fist.

"Bastard!" Whitney croaked.

"You're too friggin' drunk!" Floyd yelled.

"You'll get what you friggin' deserve!"
Selmar snarled.

Now the half-breed bent at the knees
slightly, as his left hand streaked forward from
his face while the right delved into the hair at
the nape of his neck. Something glowed red in
one hand, and something else glinted like silver
in the other. Whitney snatched his right fist
back down from out of mid-air and tried to
knock aside one of Edge's hands while with his
left he aimed a punch at the taller man's belly.
But the hand with the tiny spot of glowing red
between two of its knuckles came too fast and
packed too much strength to be deflected. It
did not impact with great force, though—just
delivered a stab of excruciating pain as the
cigarette butt burned the sensitive skin of
Whitney's right eyelid. And the pain and the
shock acted to take the power out of the blow
he landed with his own left hand.

Instinctively then, terrifyingly unsure of
whether or not the cigarette had been pushed
into his actual eye, Whitney screamed and
sought to explore the area of the agony with
the hand that had failed to defeat the searing
attack. But found the wrist of that hand
suddenly captured in a brutally tight grip, was
aware of Edge's free hand moving in a blur of
speed and next felt a warm wetness on his arm
as he was released—and had the chance he
needed to explore the cigarette burn. But in so
doing, with his good eye he saw the blood that

was pumping from the bone deep cut across the inside of his right wrist.

"You sneaky bastard!" he shrieked. "That weren't fair! Clark, the sonofabitch burned me and stuck me! Look what he friggin' done!"

Whitney covered his burned left eye with his left hand while his right one frenetically shifted its terror-filled gaze from the slashed wrist, to Edge, to Selmar and back again. And his face was almost as white as his hair as he staggered back to lean against the wall to one side of the batwing entrance: where a bunch of stunned people had gathered to stare in silence at the doubly-injured cowpuncher and the man who had hurt him.

"That was one of the most disgraceful things I ever did see!" the rancher gasped.

"Look on the bright side, feller," Edge said evenly, and commanded the attention of the entire audience as he wiped spots of blood off the blade of the razor on to the sleeve of his sheepskin coat before he replaced it in the pouch. "You could have gone for your gun and got your throat cut instead."

"I didn't go for my gun on account of I figure I ain't no match for you in that kinda showdown!" Whitney said bitterly, sagging against the wall.

Edge nodded. "Yeah, I ain't never been much with my fists."

"You're a mean bastard and no mistake!" the tall and thin Floyd accused as he waited for Edge to pass, then moved across the saloon en-

trance behind the half-breed—ripping off his
kerchief to use as a tourniquet on the injured
man's arm. "If you'd fought fair, Whitney
would have beat you real easy! He used to fight
in the booths for a livin'!"

"Damn right," the smaller C-bar-S man said
with a grimace as the kerchief was knotted
tightly to stanch the flow of blood.

"Show's over, folks," Edge told the group at
the doorway as he pushed the batwings open.
And, as the people backed off to allow him
across the threshold, he glanced over his
shoulder to say: "In a booth, uh?"

"Right!" Floyd snapped, not looking up from
his attentions to Whitney.

"Explains why he's so keen on fair fighting."

Chapter Twelve

The half-breed ordered a beer and a bottle of whiskey from the anxious-to-please bartender and carried them to a table in the darkest corner of the saloon. Where he sat down with his back to the corner and took the beer at two swallows. Then half filled the glass with whiskey and began to sip the liquor, seemingly oblivious to anything that was not in the middle distance of his surroundings as the violently interrupted social activity of the place got back to normal.

But, in fact, the newly bathed and shaved man in the damp and crumpled sheepskin coat and Stetson hat missed little of the sights and sounds that took place within range of his sensory awareness: as Whitney was hurried off by Selmar and Floyd to see the Fallon doctor while the talking and the drinking and the smoking and the card playing and, finally, the guitar strumming all got under way again. Tentatively at first, with many surreptitious glances toward the impassive-faced man at the corner table. But soon Edge was ignored and it

was almost as if there had never been any
trouble to disturb the nightly routine of the
Fallon citizens who chose to take their ease at
the end of a day's work in the Palace Saloon—
there was just the arc of unused tables and
empty chairs between the lone stranger and
the rest of the patrons to reveal that all was not
as usual tonight.

Edge did not sip too often at the liquor in the
tumbler—drank little more than what
amounted to a single shot while he waited for
the woman and remained unsure of what he
should do when she showed up. Certain only
that it was the right thing to wait for her here
in a public place rather than to go wherever
Silas Reeves had taken her.

And so he was clear-headed, the cool beer and
the fiery whiskey having honed a fresh sharp-
ness on his mind by the time the couple came
through the batwings. And to the glinting slits
of his hooded eyes she looked even better than
he remembered her—with her torso and even
her arms provocatively displayed by the tight-
ness of the bodice of her pure white dress while
from the waist down to her ankles the fullness
of the skirt was just as stirring to a man who
had seen what was concealed. Her oval face
with its blue eyes, snub nose and laughing
mouth within the frame of the honey-colored
hair was certainly more beautiful than he had
ever seen it before. She even moved with more
feminine grace. A woman fulfilled and so truly
a woman as she was escorted between the

crowded tables from the doorway to the bar.
Joyfully happy on the arm of the man who had
performed this transformation on her. A young
man who was perhaps not yet thirty and so
could well be ten years her junior. Tall and
broad and muscular from his trade of blacksmith and wheelwright. With a head of curly
black hair that hung down over the brow and
encroached a little across the leather-textured
cheeks of his round, handsome, dark-eyed, arro-
gantly confident face. The man looking a little
ridiculous, the half-breed was tempted to think,
in an out-of-fashion suit that he had outgrown
and probably did not wear very often.

But then Edge checked such a thought because it was obviously triggered by a stab of
soured jealousy he had no right to feel for Silas
Reeves as the man relished the envious looks of
several of his male fellow citizens and some re-
criminatory glowers directed at him by a few
Fallon women who knew they were put in the
shade by the aristocratic features and manner
of Helen Rochford. And he, of all men, had no
right to begrudge Reeves this woman—for had
he not been given his chance?

"Set 'em up, pal!" the powerfully built blacksmith yelled raucously above the less strident
sounds of the Palace Saloon. "Rye whiskey for
me and champagne for the little lady! It's my
lucky day and I'm in the mood for
celebration!"

"Me, too!" the Englishwoman added.
"Today is the first day of the rest of my life!

And what a bloody better life I intend to make
it than the last one! Everybody here will have a
drink! You and you and you and you and . . ."

The entrance of the couple into the saloon
had subdued the noise and then the voice of
Silas Reeves had muted it further. Now Helen
Rochford commanded utter silence as she
started to yell the annoucement, and then
climbed on to a chair with the seeming intent of
stabbing a forefinger at every patron of the
place. And gave the impression of being drunk
already—but on happiness instead of liquor—
until she pointed and looked toward the dark
corner where Edge sat; and did a double take as
her voice trailed off into the surrounding
silence of the warm, smoke-layered and abruptly tension-filled room. Her naturally pale face
now looked drained and sick and she vented a
low, strangled moan as she swayed—might
well have toppled off the chair had not two men
powered upright from a nearby table and
steadied her—each grasping a wrist and splay-
ing a hand to her waist.

While Reeves was briefly unaware of Helen
Rochford's near collapse—his entire concentration fixed upon the man who had captured her
terrified attention—stared fixedly with hatred
and contempt at Edge who continued to sit at
the corner table, both hands around the
tumbler in front of him. Until he heard the
urgent sounds of the men lunging up to keep
her from falling. And he snapped his head
around to see what was happening. Saw the

woman was in the strong and safe hands of two of the C-bar-S cowpunchers and bellowed at her:

"He's one of them, ain't he? He's one of the scum that took you by force and marked you up and—"

"No, Silas!" she shrieked, and wrenched her wrists free of the men's grip. Then leapt down off the chair as the Fallon blacksmith whirled around to face Edge again. This as one of the cowpunchers rasped an obscenity, and failed to snatch back the Colt sixshooter Reeves had slid from his holster.

And the second C-bar-S man realized the kind of mistake that was being made, so snarled: "You're wrong, Reeves!"

These words were spoken against a sudden upsurge of sound as other voices were raised. And footfalls hit the floor to the accompaniment of crashing chairs and tables and smashing glass as people struggled frantically to get clear of the line of fire.

Then two gunshots cracked out, exploded so close together they could not be separated. And in their wake there was a stretched second of solid silence while the acrid taint of black powder smoke attacked every nostril as nobody moved a muscle—even to breathe.

Until this brief period of time, elongated out of all proportion by the shock of this new and worse violence, was ended by Silas Reeves saying: "Wrong?"

There was blood on his suit jacket in the area

of his heart. And a look of tragic disbelief on
his handsome face as he stood with both hands
down at his side—the revolver still held loosely
in the right one—looking across a twenty-foot
area of abandoned tables and overturned chairs
at where Edge stood in the corner, a tumbler a
quarter full with whiskey in his left hand and a
Frontier Colt still levelled in the other, thumb
resting on the hammer and forefinger curled to
the trigger.

"Right, feller."

"Oh, God!" Silas Reeves gasped, and released the gun that had exploded a bullet into the
wall high and wide of where the half-breed
stood. Then the glaze of death came into his
dark eyes and he crashed on his knees to the
floor with a sound almost as loud as the
revolver had made. After which he started to
topple forward, but his chest hit a chair and he
was sent sprawling to the side.

By which time Edge had swallowed the
contents of the tumbler, set down the glass,
thumbed open the loading gate of his Colt and
extracted the spent shellcase. And then the
tiny sound of the case pinging on to the table
top triggered a wave of words surging from
almost every mouth. But nothing was said by
either the impassive half-breed or the terror-
stricken Englishwoman as they gazed fixedly
at each other, until Edge had reloaded the
empty chamber of the Colt with a bullet taken
from his gunbelt and slid the revolver back in
the holster. When, coming out from behind the

table—and remembering to pick up the bottle of rye as an afterthought—he came close enough to her to be heard above the hubbub of other talk and asked:

"What's somebody like you doing in a nice place like this?"

With his free hand he gripped her upper left arm. She made a token effort to struggle, but realized it was a futile gesture and submitted to him turning her around and steering her back towards the door. This as the noise was subdued again and once more the press of curious and shocked people parted to leave a path among them.

"You really are a bastard of the first order, aren't you!" she said grimly, staring straight ahead.

"And you're a first-class bitch, lady," he countered evenly, needing to suppress the arousal he felt from merely holding her by the arm as her perfume drove the odors of the saloon from his nostrils. To an extent where the bite of the chill night air struck almost icy on his exposed flesh as it dried the beads of salt moisture that had squeezed from his pores.

"And they say it is opposites that attract," she said dully as the batwings flapped closed behind them, on a saloon that was suddenly filled with movement as the people clustered around the newly dead man on the floor.

"Seems to me," Edge answered as he headed across the intersection, aware of noise and activity and a higher level of light on the surrounding streets, "that anything in pants is different enough for you."

"If the time and the place and the mood are right, why not?" she countered in the same lackluster tone as she continued to submit to the pressure of the pace and the direction he demanded. "Life is just too short to deny oneself the good things as the opportunity occurs. As poor Silas just discovered. Although by his own account he enjoyed more than his share of—"

"What about the four fellers who raped you, lady?" he asked as they approached the hotel with the disabled wagon parked out front, while the people made curious by the double gunshots gathered before the Palace Saloon.

"Where are they?" she demanded, and gave a first display of emotion since Edge brought her out of the saloon—came to an abrupt halt and turned and tilted her head to stare bitterly into his Stetson-shadowed face.

"I lost them."

She was momentarily deflated and dejected again. Then generated sufficient depth of feeling to spread a scowl across her face and put a rasp in her voice as she muttered: "That was different entirely. They took me without my consent. And even had they not hurt me physically they would still have caused me pain. Only a woman could understand how much."

He urged her on toward the sparsely lit Fallon House Hotel again and as she willingly complied, countered: "And maybe only a man who's loved a woman can understand how much another man can get hurt by the woman he loves putting out for any—"

"Geoffrey a man!" she blurted as they reached the rear of the jacked-up wagon and she suddenly wrenched her arm free of his grip and bolted up the steps on to the stoop of the building. "Do you think . . . didn't he tell you . . . why, Geoffrey Rochford is no more a man than a—"

"He told me, lady," the half-breed cut in on the shrilly shrieking Englishwoman whose face in the light through the glass panels of the double doors shone with tears. "I didn't ask. And I don't figure the town of Fallon has any right to know."

She grasped the knobs of the door and wrenched them open—snarled as she plunged into the small lobby: "I hate you, Edge!"

The half-breed started up the steps and called after her as he crossed the threshold: "He believes I'm the first man you tried to—"

She was on the stairs, and made an effort to keep her voice low and lacking in emotion as she told him: "Why don't you go about the business Geoffrey entrusted to you instead of meddling in that which you are too damn moral to truly make your personal concern?"

Helen Rochford ran up the rest of the stairs, but slowed and lightened her tread along the landing. And the sound of her opening and

closing the door of room seven was no louder
than Rosie Shay made in cracking open the
door of her private quarters.

"I heard the shootin', mister." she called in a
harsh whisper. "Trouble for you, I guess?"

"I had to kill the local ladykiller, lady," he
answered as he stepped off the threshold and
closed the door at his back.

"Oh, no." She sighed, then added: "An affair
of the heart if I ain't mistaken?"

"He was and that's where he got it."

Chapter Thirteen

Rosie Shay extended a tacit invitation to Edge by opening her door a little wider, but after glancing indifferently at her as he crossed the small lobby he remained tight-lipped as he started up the stairs.

"Reckon I might as well lock up," she said disconsolately. "And turn out the lamp. Way business is, a person can't afford to burn oil when ain't nobody around to—"

"Figure your local lawman will be by soon, lady," Edge cut in on the rambling voice of the woman who was talking for the sake of it.

She sighed and closed her door as he reached the top of the stairs and entered his room, without giving a thought to the couple who were behind the door immediately across the landing. The cramped, spartanly furnished room was filled with cold air that was also tainted with damp from the saddle and bedroll he had earlier dumped on the floor just inside the door. He considered briefly eating some kind of meager supper from the diminished supplies in his saddlebags but decided against it.

"You're getting flabby in the gut as well as the brain, feller," he told himself as he went to the bed, sat on it, swung his legs onto it and leaned his back against the headboard. He was still fully dressed, from riding boots to Stetson.

Just for a moment—a shorter time than he had thought about eating out of his saddlebag —he held the bottle of rye in one hand while the other was draped over the top of its corked neck. And grimaced into the cold and damp darkness as he recalled the impulse that had gripped him when he swept up the bottle off the table after he killed the hapless blacksmith —when he had fleetingly envisioned the Englishwoman and himself in this very room. Which was not cold and damp. Nor were they fully dressed. The bottle was uncorked and soon was empty. And there was no feeling of guilt if he happened to recall his self-conscious act of checking that Geoffrey Rochford was comfortably unconscious before he set off to find the man's wife with a firm resolve to get her away from the local stud—and a lack of confidence in his ability to reject her again. Unsure, even, if he would be able to resist the compulsion to make the advances himself.

"But you made it, feller," he told himself softly. And uncorked the bottle, raised it and growled: "Here's to you, feller. Too damn moral for your own peace of mind. Too damn moral to have yourself a piece of somebody else's."

His teeth were exposed in a sardonic grin and they showed up starkly white in the meager light which filtered in through the uncurtained window: but the glittering slivers of his narrowed eyes were brighter as they expressed an odd combination of cynicism and disillusionment. That gradually mellowed toward dispassionate resignation as the level of whiskey in the bottle fell and the quantity in his empty stomach increased. Then he drained the final heeltap of liquor as he heard the front doors of the hotel open: and continued to hold the bottle's smooth curve to his cheek as he listened to other sounds—the rap of a fist on wood, the opening of another door, the indistinct exchange of words between a man and a woman, footfalls rising on the stairway, moving along the landing and then the rap of a fist on wood again.

"It's not locked, sheriff," Edge called flatly.

The medium-built, running-to-fat, middle-aged man with the peace-officer's badge pinned to the breast pocket of his suit jacket swung open the door. And, in silhouette on the dim backdrop of light that came up from the lobby, it was plain to see Jack O'Rouke was nervously tense—maybe poised to go for the gun he carried in a shoulder holster. But the half-breed could not be sure if the lawman actually sighed his relief as the tension left him and he stepped into the room, closed the door gently behind him and leaned against it, his hands clasped at the base of his belly as if as a token of his intention to remain non-aggressive. Asked in his cultured, New England voice:

"Are you drunk, Edge?"

"With a bottle of whiskey and no grub inside me, I should be. But I guess it's been a too long day and I'm too tired."

"You may sleep here for what remains of the night."

"Intend to."

"Both incidents at the Palace Saloon were provoked by the others involved. I learned this from witnesses who, if they were partisan, would support Whitney Turner and Silas Reeves. But the fact cannot be ignored that, if you were not in Fallon, there would have been no trouble."

"Story of my life, sheriff," Edge said flatly, and dropped the bottle noisily on the floor, where it rolled under the bed. Then he took out the makings.

"I told you how Otis Selmar got this town started as little more than his ranch and some places for his hands and their families to live and spend their time when they weren't working. Since then, it's grown slowly but well. Not everybody here depends upon the C-bar-S ranch for a living anymore. But most people in Fallon share in the same ambition that Clark Selmar inherited from his father—to develop our community into a city with a fine reputation that will get it considered for capital when the territory is accepted for statehood.

"That's a long way off, we all know. But it's never too early to lay plans for something so important."

Edge lit the cigarette with a match struck on the butt of his Frontier Colt. Dropped the match to the floor.

"I can't recall the last time I planned for anything important, sheriff."

"We're lucky. We don't get very much trouble here from outsiders. So we're happy to be off the beaten track of the main trail for the present. Even the four men who are locked in the jailhouse did not happen to rustle on C-bar-S range by chance. Hayden once worked for Clark Selmar, before he was fired for laziness. Obviously he has harbored a grudge. But, unfortunately for Hayden and his partners-in-crime, he was seen and recognized by Floyd Cassidy. Which was unfortunate for you, too."

"I can't recall the last time I had a stroke of good fortune, sheriff," Edge paraphrased his last comment, the cigarette hardly moving at the corner of his mouth.

"Mrs. Rochford is the woman they are alleged to have assaulted?"

"You know it."

"And Rochford hired you to find the rapists?"

"Right."

Now O'Rouke definitely sighed. "I can understand your feelings over this conflict of interests in the prisoners, Edge. And I appreciate your attitude."

"But you don't trust it?" the half-breed posed as embarrassment seemed to check the lawman.

"Not me," O'Rouke responded quickly. "From what I have seen of you, and heard about you, I consider you to be a man of honor according to your own lights. Your word given is your word kept. But there are some in Fallon who have their doubts. Not so much about you on your own—but you in concert with Mrs. Rochford."

It seemed that he was disconcerted by his subject again, and on the verge of faltering in what he was saying. But then he hurried on, changing tack. "The frontier has not yet reached the Pacific Ocean, Edge. And Fallon has little claim to being anything but a frontier town. Nothing more than values, perhaps. But by having those values, certain citizens are inclined to mistrust strangers who do not conform immediately to . . . Goddamnit, I think you understand me, Edge. I have a job to do and I'm required to do it irrespective of whether I agree with the people who elected me. I've been instructed to instruct you to leave Fallon before noon tomorrow."

"Just like unwelcome strangers are asked to get out of frontier towns that don't claim to be—"

"I've done what I was told," O'Rouke interrupted dully, and unclasped his hand so he could reach behind him and open the door. "On my own account, I'd like to add that it might

be as well if you persuaded the Rochfords to go
with you. Since Doc McCall has said there is
nothing that he can do medically for the man.
And if the woman wishes to seek retribution
against my prisoners, she must do so by means
of legal representations in Tucson—as I think I
mentioned to you earlier."

Not a single sound from outside the room
had intruded into it since the lawman entered
and closed the door at his back. So that now,
the crash of another door as it flew open to
impact with a wall perhaps sounded dispropor-
tionately loud. From out on the street and diag-
onally across it. No ordinary door opened to
allow a person through—its nature and the
reason for its forceful opening revealed a
moment later. When galloping hooves beat on
the street: the horse raced out of the Fallon
House Hotel livery stable and passed the hotel
itself, heading for the intersection with the
main street.

Edge came up off the bed and O'Rouke
lunged away from the door. Reached the window both together—in time to glimpse a
slightly-built rider dressed all in white astride
the galloping mount a moment before the field
of vision from the window was restricted by the
frame. But as they straightened up, the half-
breed and the lawman were able to hear the
clattering hoofbeats still and knew the animal
had been steered left at the intersection, to
head along the northwestern length of Fallon's
main street.

"It was the Rochford woman," O'Rouke said.

"I wouldn't bet against it."

"She has a rifle and she's heading for the jail-house."

The hoofbeats were getting fainter in the distance, but they could still be heard clearly enough for the men at the window of the hotel room to distinguish the fact that the horse was being slowed.

"That direction sure enough."

O'Rouke stared fixedly out into the dark night, as if struggling to see over and through the intervening buildings to where he knew the red-brick building with the barred windows and the gallows in the yard out back was sited. And an anguished expression was abruptly spread across his deeply lined and weather-darkened face as the clatter of hooves on hard-packed dirt was curtailed.

"You don't think ... ?" he started in a tone of voice that announced he knew he was clutching at straws that didn't even exist.

Silence crowded into the void that followed the end of what he was saying—a silence that was generated by more than just the two men in this room straining to hear what was to come in the wake of the reining to a halt of the horse. Like the whole town was holding its collective breath. Then a man cried out. Too far off for what he yelled to be understood—so that Edge and O'Rouke knew only that the man experienced terror. Before a fusillade of gunfire exploded. Reached the hotel room after travelling the same distance, but sounding loud enough to mask whatever lesser noise was created in any part of town in reaction to the exploding of the hail of shots. Twelve of them in all, spaced equally apart by the need to pump the action of the repeater so that an empty shellcase was ejected and a fresh bullet was jacked into the breech after each squeezing of the trigger. Until the magazine was exhausted, when there was another period of silence as stretched seconds were linked together: before hoofbeats hit the distant street once more. Receding into the distance.

"Yeah, I sometimes think more than's good for me, sheriff," Edge said to the lawman who looked like he had felt a shockwave from every bullet that exploded from the muzzle of the repeater rifle. "But I figure that can be better than talking too much."

Now, it sounded like the whole town was shouting demands for its questions to be answered. This as many shafts of light were laid out into the night by newly lit lamps, and Edge opened the window to arc the butt of his cigarette across the balcony and down on to the street.

"Those men were unarmed and locked in cells," O'Rouke groaned. "Helpless."

"Helen Rochford was naked and alone when she stumbled on their camp. If she had had some help—"

"Goddamnit, there's no room for that kind of

thinking anymore!" the lawman snarled, whirling from the window and swinging around the end of the bed to reach the door. Which he wrenched open before he added bitterly: "We Fallon people are striving to put behind us that eye-for-an-eye morality!"

He had to swerve suddenly to avoid crashing into Geoffrey Rochford who stood on the landing, the blanket draped over his shoulders serving only partially to conceal his nakedness.

"Help me, I beg of you!" the Englishman pleaded, thrusting out an exploring hand and failing to make contact with the hurrying sheriff. "What is happening? Please help me? I can't see."

"Me neither, feller," the half-breed growled as he moved at a far easier pace in the wake of O'Rouke. "In the matter of eye to eye with some people."

"Edge?" Rochford croaked, turning away from the sound of the sheriff's footfalls and reaching toward the sound of a familiar voice while his other hand continued to clutch the blanket at his throat. He took an anxious step forward and something akin to a smile of immense relief made a tentative visit to his pale-under-the-tan, dead-eyed face. "Is that you, Mr. Edge?"

"Ain't been myself lately, but I figure it is," the half-breed answered, taking hold of the outstretched hand as if he were going to shake it. Then he pushed the hand and arm down to the side of the man as Rochford vented a short gust of laughter.

"Helen has gone again, Edge! Do you know where? Will you help me to find her? Do you know where she is? Dear God, I feel so utterly useless without eyes."

"No sweat, feller. Figure we have to have a better chance than the rest of getting to her first," Edge answered, and took a hold of Rochford's wrist to turn the man and steer him back into his room across the landing.

"Better chance than the rest? I don't understand. Better chance than the rest, Mr. Edge? Are you telling me we are in competition with others in seeking Helen?"

"The enlightened people of this town, feller," the half-breed answered evenly as he eased the Englishman into a seated posture on the bed. "But, like I say, it's better to come from the blind side."

Chapter Fourteen

Edge needed to light the lamp on the bureau in room seven to find Geoffrey Rochford's clothes, which he piled on the bed beside the Englishman—ignoring his constant barrage of questions which demanded an explanation of the cryptic comment with regard to Helen being sought by others. Inquiries made it apparent the man was still unconscious during the slaughter at the jailhouse—had come to amid the raucous shouting of the townspeople.

"I should be ashamed of myself making bad jokes about blindness, feller," the half-breed said at length, silencing the Englishman's vain interrogation and talking over a buzz of voices from another part of Fallon. "I'll tell you about it later. For now, get your threads on and wait for me. What I have to do will take more than a couple of minutes. I'll be back."

He grasped Rochford's hand again and moved it to rest on the pile of clothes beside him.

"You will bring Helen back here to the

hotel?" the Englishman asked eagerly, and reached out to try to maintain a physical contact with Edge after the half-breed pulled away.

"No."

He turned out the lamp in the blind man's room before he left it to recross the landing and enter his own which was already in darkness. Draped his bedroll over one shoulder and hefted his saddle under the other arm to carry the gear downstairs. Geoffrey Rochford called out: "Thanks for what you are doing for me," and Edge made no response. He felt cold air coming up from the lobby and saw the reason for this was the open doorway.

Rosie Shay stepped in from the stoop, hugging herself in the topcoat draped over her shoulders but still shivering. "Goodness, what a thing to have happened?" she said rhetorically. "I only went to the corner, but they say the jail is a charnel house. Blood all over the place. All four rustlers as dead as poor Harry. But at least he died peacefully. He wasn't slaughtered. What if there had been other prisoners in the cells? A drunk or someone like that? Imagine that? And the woman was stayin' here in my hotel."

"Silas Reeves, ma'am?" Edge said.

"Oh, that was self-defense, the way I was told about—"

"Obliged if you'd tell me where I can find his workshop."

"Workshop? Oh, I see. Yeah, if you turn

right outside and go down to the intersection
and across it, the place where he worked is
three blocks down. On the right. Has the name
Reeves' Forge painted on the doors.''

"Obliged to you. I'll see you about the room
rent when I get back."

She went to the door that gave onto her
private quarters while Edge moved to the ones
she had left open. And she called after him as
he stepped out on to the stoop:

"You oughta have taken up my invite,
mister. Once a whore always a whore—special-
ly when she's a widow. And a man always
knows where he is with a whore."

Perhaps the lonely and frustrated hotel
keeper continued to speak in the same dull
tone, but she had to know she was talking to
herself after Edge had stepped down off the
stoop. Where he paused briefly to toss his gear
over the tailgate into the rear of the disabled
wagon. Then he followed Rosie Shay's directions through a section of town that was quiet
again—the center of activity having moved to
the area of the jailhouse. While many of those
too timid to gravitate toward the scene of the
mass killings looked out from darkened windows at the tall, lean, loose-limbed half-breed
as he strode purposefully but without haste to
the intersection and across it. He sensed the
watching eyes and once heard a whispered
exchange that was patently resentful in tone.

Fallon being the kind of town it was, the
double doors of the blacksmith forge and

wagon repair shop were not locked. Edge
struck a match to get his bearings within the
building that was as cluttered on the inside as
it was ramshackle outside. As he had expected,
Silas Reeves had been too busy with other pur-
suits to start in on fixing the badly buckled
wheel off the Rochfords' wagon. But the useless wheel provided a pattern from which he
was able to locate one of the same size from a
stock of new ones. He needed to strike four
more matches before he found what he was
looking for—and by then the acrid smell of
burning had masked a far subtler aroma that
was in the chill atmosphere of the crowded and
untidy workshop. Or maybe, he reflected
briefly as he rolled the wheel back through the
forge and out over the threshold, he only
imagined he had caught the scent of the
Englishwoman's perfume: triggered by a
glimpse of a rumpled bed in a corner of the
cluttered room.

As he rolled the wheel back the way he had
come, he guessed he was under surveillance
again. And maybe there was talk about him.
But the wheel was heavy and an awkward size
for a man of his build to roll smoothly. The
weariness that had kept him from getting
drunk now weighed more heavily on his eyelids
and seemed to make every muscle in his frame
ache. And the whiskey that had left him sober
felt like it was still sloshing about his stomach,
getting more sour by the moment. Thus he
needed to concentrate his entire attention on

steering the wheel, denying his need for rest
and fighting the threat of nausea—which left
no part of his perception free to monitor his
surroundings. Until he had fitted the new
wheel to the wagon, fixed it firmly on the axle
and leaned against the rim to take a few moments of rest: flexing his shoulder, arm and
hand muscles. Only a long period of sleep
would cure his tiredness, but at least the
danger of throwing up had passed—and the
relief he felt at this was matched by the easing
of tension he detected in the atmosphere
around him. Which made itself silently and in-
visibly even more evident as he crossed to the
hotel livery and brought out the two mules—
the only animals left in the stable after Helen
Rochford took the chestnut gelding.

Just as he completed putting the mules in
the traces of the wagon, the doors of the Fallon
House Hotel opened and Rosie Shay emerged,
talking softly as she gently led Geoffrey Rochford out on to the stoop. He was fully and
neatly dressed in the expensive suit and this
served to emphasize the sick-looking, skull-like
gauntness of his bristled face with the starkly
white bandage across his brow.

"Edge?" he asked.

"He's fixed the wheel and now he's puttin'
the mules to the wagon, Mr. Rochford," the
full-bodied, no longer over-painted woman supplied.

"All ready to leave, feller?" the half-breed

asked as he moved to the front of the stoop steps.

"I needed help. Mrs. Shay provided it. She told me what happened. What Helen did."

"She likes to talk more than I do," Edge said and went up the steps to take over the task of guiding the blinded Englishman as, in the distance, the hooves of several horses beat at the ground—lunged from a standstill to an immediate gallop. "How much do I owe, ma'am?"

"This gentleman settled all accounts, mister," Rosie Shay answered as she surrendered with a frown of reluctance her grip on Rochford's arm.

"Your bill was little enough, sir, and I will not take it from the fee that was agreed."

Edge's only response was to tell Rochford when to step down. Then gave him even-voiced instructions that enabled him to climb aboard the wagon and lower himself securely on the passenger's side of the seat. After this, Edge climbed up and sat on the driver's side. Touched his hat brim and nodded to the woman on the stoop as he kicked off the brakes and flicked the reins.

"Goodbye, Mrs. Shay, and thank you so very much," the Englishman called in his cultured tones as the wagon jolted slightly in coming off the blocks and was steered into a tight turn.

"Good luck to you, mister!" she answered. "And I reckon you sure deserve it after you had so much of the bad kind!"

Eyes watched from secret places again while the clop of hooves, creak of timbers and clatter of the wheel-rims masked every whispered word that was spoken as the rig rolled by.

"I left some money with Mrs. Shay to cover the services of the local doctor, Edge," the rigidly seated, fixedly face-forward Englishman said as the wagon crossed the intersection. "Do I owe anybody else for anything that was done for me or Helen while I was not conscious? Or for you?"

"You have two dollars, feller?"

Eagerly anxious to provide what was needed, Rochford quickly delved a hand into an inside pocket of his suit jacket and took out a sheaf of bills. Invited: "Take it. And please take something on account of what you are owed. I know I do not have the full—"

"Just a couple of bucks for now," Edge cut in as he reined the mules to halt the rig outside the still open doorway of the forge. "Pay for the wheel."

Already familiar with the layout of the place, the half-breed did not need to light his way into the forge of the dead Silas Reeves, where he left the money under a horseshoe on an anvil. Then, up on the seat alongside Geoffrey Rochford, it was necessary to turn the wagon again: to head back along the street and swing across the intersection.

"Are you sure that is all, sir?" the Englishman asked at length. "What about Helen? Did she not incur any—"

There was just a small knot of Fallon citizens outside the dimly-lit jailhouse now. Clustered around a flatbed wagon on which four burlap-wrapped forms were already loaded, neatly side by side. The half-breed recognized none of the townspeople, and the corpses had been shrouded in such a way that it was impossible to distinguish between Arch Hayden and Leroy Engels, Sonny the kid and Toby the black man.

"No sweat, feller," Edge assured evenly as the wagon rolled on by the stationary one. "Your wife paid them all back."

Chapter Fifteen

Edge drove the wagon slowly through the night and into the morning. Cold, tired, hungry and in no good mood for conversation. While his passenger talked a great deal, unconcerned that he drew no vocal responses from the man beside him and resigned to the fact that he was not able to see how the half-breed silently received what was being told him. Simply grateful to have a perhaps attentive listener for what he had to say—which amounted to a denial of Rosie Shay's parting comment to him with a defense of his wife.

Maybe Geoffrey Rochford would have talked for the entire night without need to repeat any incident that proved his good fortune in persuading Helen to marry him more than adequately compensated for the bad luck that had dogged him all his life. But, as the false dawn broke, another norther swept down the broad valley. There was no rain in the dirty grey clouds that were racing across the high sky but the wind was both bitterly cold and noisily powerful. Moaned and whined against

and around every obstacle in its path—as if in
frustrated aggravation that the way was not
entirely clear. The wagon was just such an
obstacle and soon after the norther began to
blow, noise made all but shouted talk futile.
And there was the added discomfort of flying
dust and tiny pieces of vegetation that stung
the face and against which it was best to keep
the mouth closed.

In the murky first light of the new day, the
half-breed was able to take his bearings
through eyes barely cracked open to the on-
slaught of the debris-laden wind. Saw that he
was on the stretch of trail that ran past the
area of rearing rock bluffs that guarded the
deep basin where Selmar and his hands had
captured the quartet of ill-fated rustlers. And
he tugged on the reins to turn the mules off the
trail to head for one of the canyon-like gaps in
the rock wall. The trail had been relatively
smooth in contrast to the uneven pastureland
which the rig now jolted and yawed over.

"Something is wrong?" Rochford yelled.

"Just with the weather, feller! I think I know
a place where we can get out of it!"

"I am entirely in your hands, sir!"

In amongst the rocky ravines the sounds of
the wind were louder and eerie. Likewise when
the wagon emerged on to the lodge to come to
one side of the natural amphitheater and Edge
and the Englishman could hear the norther as
it tore through the pines that grew thickly to
the very rim of the far side of the basin. The

true dawn had broken by then and with less
dust being raised and thrown through the gust-
ing air Edge was able to see clearly down into
the massive crater: and he drew back his lips to
display a grin of satisfaction as he saw he had
been right to come here. That this weird place
which yesterday had created such odd effects
with sound in a surrounding stillness was this
morning serene in the same tranquility below
the rim as had existed when he was first here.
Then there had been a column of smoke from
the rustler's fire to exhibit the full extent of the
perfect quiescence of the bottom land. Whereas
now there was just the unmoving trees and
brush to show what it was like down there
while up here anything that was not rock-solid
was shaken and swayed and bent to the forceful dictates of the norther.

Then, after yelling at Rochford to hold tight
because of a steep downgrade, Edge urged the
mules off the rock ledge and on to the grassy
slope: steering the animals over a zig-zag route
that was the easiest way but still needing to
hold the wagon with the brakes more often
than the wheels ran free. As, by slow degrees,
the many sounds of the wind became lower in
volume after it had ceased to buffet the wagon.

"God, what a relief," the Englishman said at
length, speaking an an almost reverent whisper
that produced no eerie echo while the norther
continued to rage across the basin. "What is
this place? How did you find it?"

"Another time, maybe," Edge replied wearily as the wagon reached the flat base of the crater and he hauled on the reins and locked on the brakes to halt the rig. "Been a long time since I slept and unless I get me some—"

"Oh, I'm terribly sorry, sir. I never realized—"

"No way you could have known, feller," the half-breed interrupted him. "Sit tight for awhile, until I get a camp set up."

"Whatever you say."

It took the half-breed some thirty minutes to do what was necessary—take the mules from the traces and hobble them, gather kindling and fuel and light a fire on the ashes of the old one, break out his gear from the rear of the wagon and unfurl his bedroll with his saddle positioned to serve as a pillow. Then he stood at the side of the wagon and explained to the patient Englishman:

"Animals are taken care of, there's a fire and I'm going to bed down alongside it. You want to be near the fire, or maybe you want to stretch out on the bed in the back of the wagon?"

While Edge had prepared the camp, Rochford had listened hard to all the sounds he made—and moved his head as if to gaze at him with the sightless dark eyes beneath the bandage that was now as grey with dust as everything else about the men and the wagon.

Listening to the half-breed talk to him, the
Englishman faced directly to the front and
nodded several times. Then answered:

"When I decide what to do, I shall do it, sir. I
wish you to go to your rest and leave me to my
own devices. After all, there is a chance I will
never regain my vision. And so the sooner I
begin trying to fend for myself, the better."

"Okay, feller."

"I'm most grateful."

Edge moved into the area of warmth emanat-
ed by the fire and removed only the sheepskin
coat and the Stetson. Shared the shelter of his
blankets and the coat with the uncocked Winchester and blotted out the sight of the scudding grey clouds and the swaying trees above
the basin's rim with the hat over his face.
Wanted to respond to what the Englishman
called to him, but the need for sleep was
greater—and forced itself upon him as Rochford finished saying:

"For I know you are making no effort to find
Helen, Edge. Yet."

His sleep was uncharacteristically sound. Of a
kind that only near-total physical and mental
exhaustion could bring to a man like Edge:
hovering him on the very brink of unconsciousness. A dreamless sleep—although during the
moments of coming awake he was disconcert-
ingly disorientated and he thought the sounds
he heard were the remnants of audible images

that had been troubling his sleeping mind while he was oblivious to reality.

"Edge?" a man said in the tone of a demand, that seemed to echo without being repeated. "Something is happening."

The brittle words were spoken in competition with the crackling of a good fire and were accompanied by a dragging sound: all heard against an utter, almost palpable silence. And the waking man recalled where he was and why he was there. Felt warm and well rested and ravenously hungry. Then experienced a sense of relief that the norther had finished blowing, as he pushed his hat on the top of his head and sat up to say to the Englishman:

"Easy, feller."

But then was far from easy in his own mind— when he blinked against the glaring light of a cloud-scattered but sun-bright late-morning sky and saw the menacing situation which the blinded man had sensed: or maybe had heard as it developed.

In the immediate area of the campsite, little had changed with the weather since Edge went quickly to sleep in the early morning. The fire had been kept burning warmly to combat the winter cold that was little relieved by the sun. And Geoffrey Rochford had needed to climb down off the wagon and moved cautiously to find fresh fuel and feed the flames with it. Had gathered more than would ever be needed and this was piled on the other side of the fire from

where Edge had bedded down. The dragging
sound was made by the Englishman as he came
around the fire from the heap of fuel—pulling
with his hands and pushing with his feet so
that he slithered along the ground on one side
of his rump. His head was turned and held
rigidly, his face toward the long slope they had
zig-zagged over to get to the bottom of the
basin. The expression on his green-eyed,
broken-nosed, pale-as-the-bandage face was of
terror of the unknown for a moment—then he
came close to smiling in relief as he halted his
move when Edge offered the misplaced re-
assurance. Misplaced, the half-breed realized,
when he raked his slit-eyed gaze away from the
brightening face of Rochford to peer in the
direction where the man sensed danger.

"You have cause not to be, I think," the
Englishman said. Still unafraid now that the
half-breed was awake, but knowing there was
probably something to be afraid of. "I'd rather
you did not try to spare my feelings, sir. For a
man who has been made suddenly blind, there
cannot be very much more . . . providing he has
somebody he can trust to act as his eyes in
times when—"

"You know we're at the bottom of a pretty
steep slope, feller," Edge cut in, continuing to
sit on the ground, half draped by blankets and
the sheepskin coat—his right hand still lightly
gripping the frame of the Winchester. "There's
a high curve of cliff on the other side of us.
Guess you've noticed that the lay of the land

does strange things to sounds. At the top of the slope there's a line of men still in their saddles. I figure they're close to a mile away from us. But they can hear every word we say. Sun's out now and they can see us real good as well."

"Not strangers?" Rochford asked, face still upturned as if he was trying by an effort of will to regain his sight so he could see for himself the scene that was being so laconically described for him.

"No, feller. The Fallon sheriff, Clark Selmar, who's the biggest rancher in the valley. Floyd Cassidy his top hand, Whitney Turner and a half dozen other C-bar-S hands I recall seeing from the last time I was here. Some men I saw at the Palace Saloon last night. Some more I don't recall. But I guess they're all Fallon people. I count nineteen men in all."

Rochford waited for a stretched second for Edge to go on. Then opened his mouth to voice a question, but was unable to start it before his wife shouted:

"And one woman, Geoffrey! I'm with them and I'm coming down! They've let me go, my darling!"

The Englishman wrenched his head from side to side—turning to look toward the sound of Helen's voice as she announced her presence and then staring sightlessly back at the half-breed. His expression implored an explanation.

Edge had dug the makings from a pocket of his shirt and now he let go of the Winchester as he stood up and began to roll a cigarette. Said as he did so:

"Yeah, and your wife, feller. Riding the chestnut gelding. She looks to be in pretty good shape. The Fallon posse is just waiting and watching."

"It's all right, my darling!" the honey-haired woman in the no-longer-quite-so-white dress called as the half-breed paused to strike a match on the butt of his holstered revolver. "The sheriff and his men caught up with me easily! But after I explained what those brutal beasts did to me . . . well, a great many of them have wives. Some have daughters. They agreed to take no action against me for what I did at Fallon, Geoffrey. They were taking me back to the town to fetch you when the smoke of your fire was seen. And the tracks of the wagon. Oh, my darling Geoffrey, it is all going to be so wonderful for us after the doctors make you see again."

There was no need for a horserider to zig-zag down the slope and Helen Rochford veered off a direct path from top to bottom only when a natural obstacle made it necessary. And, as she drew closer and became aware of the strange acoustics of the basin she dropped her voice to a normal conversational level.

"It is not a cruel trick, is it?" the Englishman asked, turning from his wife to face Edge again.

"It's no trick, Rochford!" Sheriff Jack O'Rouke yelled. "In the cold light of day it was decided your wife had sufficient provocation for what she did to be entered in the Fallon records as justifiable homicide! But I give the lady and your travelling companion fair warning! If she or Edge ever set foot within my jurisdiction again the killings in which they were involved will be reexamined!''

O'Rouke was first to jerk on the reins to wheel his horse away from the top of the slope. But the rest of the posse was quick to follow his example. The sounds of the sudden mass departure were initially loud but then were immediately curtailed as the Fallon men rode off the rock ledge and into the ravine.

"Good God!" Helen Rochford spat scornfully as she rode the gelding off the slope and across the final few yards to the campsite. "I would have to be out of my mind to even think about returning to this awful place again!"

"Help me, sir?" her husband asked, extending a hand toward Edge. "I would not wish to fall into the fire."

The half-breed gripped the wrist of the upraised arm and steered rather than pulled the blinded man to his feet. This as the woman reined the gelding to a halt and swung wearily out of the saddle. Smoothed her trail-dirtied and travel-crumpled dress with the palms of her hands and then finger-combed some of the tangles out of her hair. Smiled through the smoky heat shimmer above the fire at the two men as she made a token gesture of rubbing off

the dust that was ingrained into the pale skin
and her blue-eyed, snub-nosed face and said:

"I expect it to take at least two hours and
two bathsful of really hot water for me to be
clean and presentable again."

She found her gaze in the trap of Edge's
glinting eyes, and tried to brighten her smile in
the hope of encouraging something other than
the ice cold response from him. And only
managed to get free of the trap when her husband said softly:

"A blind man does not care what his wife
looks like, Helen."

He extended his arms with the palms of his
hands inwards and his fingers splayed: inviting
her to come to him. On his darkly bristled face
was an expression of melancholy that made it
look as if he was close to spilling tears from his
sightless eyes.

"It is nice to know that somebody is pleased
to have me safe and well and free," the woman
said bitterly. Then replaced her sour glower
with a radiant smile and injected happiness
into her voice as she came quickly away from
the horse and around the fire. "Yes, my dearest
husband. Please forgive me for the terrible
accident I caused. I promise you—"

He turned to the sound of her so that she was
able to move easily into his outstretched arms
that closed around her in an embrace. As Edge
turned, also: but to put his back to the couple
as they kissed and the woman's voice was cur-

tailed. The half-breed unsure of whether he could conceal from Helen Rochford the fact that her deliberate attempt to arouse his lusting jealousy was having an effect upon him.

"But he does care about what she is, Helen," Geoffrey Rochford said evenly after perhaps two seconds. "And you are evil. Utterly and totally evil in your selfish striving to fulfill your depraved desire to dominate men."

Edge controlled the compulsion to turn around and look at the couple as the Englishman spoke so dispassionately to his silent wife. Continued to keep his back to them as he regularly drew in smoke from the cigarette and exhaled it, thumbs hooked over the buckle of his gunbelt and narrowed, heavily hooded eyes staring fixedly into the middle distance. His mind reflecting upon every rotten thing he knew about this bitch siren of a woman—from when he first saw her as she launched a kick at the belly of a dying horse until, just a few seconds ago, she had directed the seductive smile at him—her pleasure in the sexuality of the situation enhanced by the presence of her husband who was blind to the smile and to the way she swayed her body.

"Perhaps if I were not now blind, I could have made the same allowance as before, Helen," Geoffrey Rochford went on after a brief pause during which Edge had expected the woman to launch into a shrill denial of what

her husband was saying, "when you gave yourself to man after man and I was able to forgive
you. Because you had chosen to marry me
despite what I am. And I could look at you and
placate my jealousy with pride in you."

Edge turned now. His head, then from the
waist and finally moved his feet. To lock his
eyes with those of Helen Rochford. Blue on
blue. But narrowed as opposed to wide. As the
man struggled to control an impulse to inter-
vene while the woman was slowly throttled to
death.

"But I cannot bear to be literally in the dark
while you make your pathetic attempts to pre-
tend you are faithful, my darling wife. Dear
God, you were even able to cast your evil spell
over this man Edge. To make him want you as
much as he hates you. . . ." Rochford wrenched
his head around and with his quickly acquired
ability that compensated for the loss of sight
was able to remain face to face with the silent
and unmoving half-breed as he challenged:
"Isn't that right, sir? Can you say without
truth that you never intended to search for my
wife until after you had ridden yourself of me?
Done what you could for me in order to salve
your conscience while you were looking for her
so that you could—"

"You can let go of her now, feller," Edge said
flatly.

"No! If you want to have her that much,
you'll have to kill me! Taking her away from

me won't be enough because—"

"You can only kill somebody once," Edge cut in on the man again. "And your wife is dead already."

The blinded man stood with his head turned and his mouth open for perhaps three seconds. Then turned toward the woman again, willing himself more strongly than ever to be able to see. But he was denied the sight of the blue-tinged, bulging-eyed, bloated-cheeked and protruding-tongued face of his wife above both his hands locked securely around her throat. And, below his hands, her limp body and limbs that without life also lacked sexual attraction.

"Help me?" Rochford moaned.

Edge went to the man, encircled an arm around the slender waist of the corpse and gently pulled one from the other. And, when Rochford had surrendered his supporting death hold on his wife, the half-breed lowered the burden carefully to the ground, clear of the fire.

"You could have killed me before I finished it," the Englishman said impassively as he let his arms fall loosely to his sides.

"Yeah, I could have."

"But you didn't."

"I ain't a thief, feller. Especially I don't rob the dead."

"You'll help me still, sir?"

The half-breed's cigarette had gone out and he stooped back to pick up the cold end of a burning stick. Relit the tobacco and answered: "Take you as far as Tucson and put you on the stage."

"I'll pay you four thousand dollars for that. Since you feel unable to accept it as the agreed fee for—"

"Four thousand less what Rosie Shay charged you for my room, feller. I pay my own way."

"Suit yourself, sir."

"Usually do." He moved away from the fire toward the wagon. "I'll get us ready to roll."

"Should we not eat first? Or at least have a cup of tea? A drink perhaps?"

"I'll find us a better place," Edge answered, shifting his gaze away from the corpse beside the fire and then glancing around the rim of the basin as his voice resounded off the curve of cliff.

"Just as you wish," Geoffrey Rochford allowed, and lowered himself carefully into a cross-legged posture on the ground. And remained quiet with his own thoughts, left the half-breed alone with his, until they were both back up on the seat of the wagon. The mules in the traces, the unsaddled gelding hitched on at the back and the blanket-wrapped corpse of Helen on the bed in the rear. When the Englishman ended the long silence with: "I do so appreciate all you have done for me, Edge."

"No sweat," the half-breed replied, and urged the mules into movement. Steered the team over the same zig-zag route by which they had come down the steep slope.

"I think I have an idea of just how difficult it was for you to resist the advances of my late wife, sir," the Englishman argued, staring blindly ahead. "And, who knows, a man such as you might well have been exactly what Helen needed to become a whole and fulfilled woman. Much more than all those others I always pretended I never. . . . But, of course, I am deeply gratified that you felt unable to. . . ."

He did not look grateful for anything as he sat rigidly on the seat of the jolting wagon, sightless eyes perhaps filled with remembered images of his no longer alluringly beautiful wife —while tears spilled from them to make irregular channels through the dirt and bristles on his cheeks. Edge looked at the grief-stricken man for just a second or so, before he turned his attention to the task of driving the wagon out of the basin. And murmured, softly enough for the sounds of the slow rolling wagon to mask what he said:

"Maybe one day I'll be grateful, too. But right now I'm real sorry I didn't try a little ardor."